ALWAYS THE DEAD

Stephen J. Golds

D1566409

RED DOG
UK

Published by RED DOG PRESS 2021

Paperback ISBN 978-1-914480-86-7

Ebook ISBN 978-1-914480-87-4

www.reddogpress.co.uk

For
ghosts.

Mine and yours.

This is a work of fiction based upon true events.

"All truth is crooked, time itself is a circle."
Friedrich Nietzsche

PROLOGUE

THE SAME OLD Hell. The same old horror. So bright, it looked like a star going supernova.

The film started to roll. The lights dimmed.

I was used to it. It was exhaustingly familiar. Watching the same black and white news reels in the same darkened theater on the same gloomy Sunday. I always knew the next scene. The next act.

APRIL 1ST, 1945. Easter Sunday. April Fool's Day.

Hurtling towards the coast of Okinawa again. Blue ocean again. White beaches in the distance again. The big L-Day, they had called it. Operation Iceberg, but there was no ice on the island of Okinawa. No ice water in hell.

Surrounded by the faceless Marines of a ghost battalion, a phantom platoon in an Amphibious Transport Vehicle headed for those beaches of the South Eastern side of Okinawa Island. Once these men had looked to me for guidance. Leadership. Now they were all dead. Just vacant faces in the same stark memories. They looked to me for nothing because they were dead. Movie extras playing out their parts, shuffling quietly off the set. Exit stage left.

All dead. A decomposed platoon silently singing our Marine Division's fight song, our battle hymn; A child's nursery rhyme we'd picked up from R and R in Australia.

Waltzing Matilda…

It was L-Day, and we were kids. Fear, anticipation, dread, and expectation were heavy and wet in the air, mixed with the stench of the ocean. It was palpable. Breathable. We could feel

1

it there moving in our lungs, in our guts, a watery bayonet. We thought Okinawa would be something like a rerun of the D-Day landings, something akin to Iwo Jima or Saipan, but the beaches were as empty as the Marines' faces that looked upon them. Desolate. Stark. Vacant.

We drifted slowly then. The waves crashed into the bows of the Amphibs. We watched and waited, fingering our rifles and Thompson M1 machine guns in an eternal state of waiting. The beaches motionless and very still.

Dead.

Where were the Japs? They should have been there waiting for us, giving us hell. We'd expected banzai charges, kamikaze soldiers waving samurai swords and wearing grenade vests. Machine gun fire. Mortar explosions. We had expected to shed blood. The beaches were empty, like the beaches in Kerry had been.

MY FATHER WAS a giant to me then. The sand white and soft between my toes. Five years old. The air smelt like I'd always belonged there. In the pit of my stomach. I'd always been there. My father and I searched for cockles and mussels in the white, wet sand, the surf sliding up the beach and washing over our feet. My mother would boil them for our supper that night. We were at Inch Beach in Kerry, Ireland. I was five years old. My father chuckled. He wasn't a shriveled corpse in the charity ward. He showed me shiny, black shells cupped in his palms. I showed him the Thompson machine gun in my fists.

SAND AND PALM trees and bamboo jungle on the land and hills beyond. And those cliffs. Always those cliffs.

The sound of the Amphibs' engines and the ocean a blunt deafness in this silent movie. A flock of large white birds flew up and away from a small cove. Then it began; not what we had thought. Not what we had trained for. Nothing like any of us had ever seen before. Nothing any of us would forget, the ones who lived through the coming days, weeks, months and made it back home.

I squinted into the sun. Coming to the climax of a memory. My right eye ached. Things falling from those dark cliffs into the crashing sea below. One after another. Vertical drops. Flashes of white and then nothing. Flashes of red and then again nothing.

The Amphibs' cruised closer. The cliffs grew larger. The falling, flashing shapes took form and we realized it was Jap women and children committing mass suicide. Women and children leaping silently, jumping hand-in-hand from those brown cliffs into the waves and the rocks below. Over and over again. With hollowed eyes, from the inside of the sounds of machinery and water, we watched them dive. Their bodies seemed to fall so unnaturally, so slowly before hitting the rocks and froth. A slow waltz into the abyss. And then it wasn't until I was carried close enough to make out the features of the faces, I saw it wasn't the Japs plunging to those jagged ocean deaths. It was my wife and child, jumping hand in hand. They leapt hand in hand over and over again. My daughter's golden hair braided. She had pneumonia. Screaming for her Daddy...

"Daddy! Daddy!"

And, Jean, wearing a bloody blue dress that rippled in the breeze, dying like falling in love with the ocean and the rocks.

Screaming muted; my lungs heavy with liquid and my chest loaded. Full of broken glass and dust. My throat burned like gasoline. Being eaten from the inside out. I tried to escape the Amphib', over the side. Climbing, slipping, my hands too wet. I thought it was ocean water, but it was blood. It was always blood. It had always been blood. I wanted to make them stop. *Please don't jump. Wait for me there on the edge. Wait for me there in the darkness. I'll follow you there.*

I lunged into the colorless water, tried to swim. Sink or swim. Sink or fucking swim. Waves smashed me down. I sank. I always sank. Water filled my lungs. The salt_water burned holes there. My chest filled with burning water. Drowning and blind.

"Lieutenant..."
"Lieutenant."
"Lieutenant!"

I ALWAYS KNEW when it had reached that point, that it was another night terror. Another hallucination. Things I never understood. Ruined shapes of things. A drugged cocktail of memory, shame, and regret. The meaning beyond my grasp. I didn't know anything, but I knew about drowning. I couldn't breathe. A memory: drowning, and someone shouting.

CHAPTER 1

ANOTHER WAVE OF coughing fits wrenched me gasping away from the Pacific Ocean, smashed me into my hospital bunk. The nurses rushed over. Their large, wet eyes peaked out between white fabric masks and small, white hats. Little women wearing white uniforms hiding white skin, rushing around amidst white walls, white bed sheets, and a white ceiling. For a moment, if I were a fool, I could have imagined I was trapped in heaven. But my surroundings more closely resembled purgatory, mopped clean with disinfectant and industrial soap by a spook in dirty, white overalls. The nurses examined my blood-speckled sheets and the pinkish drool on my palsied hands. They propped me up with pillows, wiped me down with a moist cloth, and brought me water in a misty glass. They seemed to smile at me through their fabric masks, brows creased with concern as my cough smoothed out a little with my breathing.

"I'm okay," I told them.

"I'm okay, damn it," I told myself.

I smiled with teeth stained red, waved them away. They took turns nodding at me, made sympathetic noises. They ran over to check on the old man named McGee with the white stubble and white hair, hacking blood, and yelling at everyone and everything in the bunk by the doorway. A diseased dog.

"Dreaming about those cliffs in the Pacific again, eh, Lieutenant?" said Sinclair, the tall, gaunt, spook who occupied the bunk next to mine.

I always called him a 'spook', but I didn't dislike him. I didn't particularly dislike Negroes. Sinclair seemed like a good guy. Most Negroes were as trustworthy or loyal as white folks. I never understood all that race-supremacy bullshit. A shit stain was still a shit stain, no matter the tint of the shit. I saw that in the war firsthand. I didn't care what color the soldier was or who was watching my back, just as long as he was watching it—not that I ever had anyone like that back in Okinawa or any other time in my life. I was a second lieutenant in the Marines, which meant I always had other backs to worry about, besides my own. Personally, I'd always preferred to be alone, especially after the war anyhow. I had been a loner in my marriage, a loner in the war, and a loner in the sanatorium; I liked it like that.

The Doc said I should try and make friends. It would help me recuperate from the illness faster. I'd become some kind of social leper, after the war—very poor communication and social skills. Pulling a trigger on people tends to change your world view. Conversation and small talk can be difficult and seem altogether worthless when you have seen how easily the human body comes apart, how simple it is to switch someone's lights out. On The Doc's orders, the best I could scrape together was a racial *tête-à-tête* with Sinclair, who had a quiet intelligence and wit about himself. A numbers runner back in the days of Dutch Schultz, he'd gone on to fight but get injured in the war over in Europe. He'd moved his family out to L.A. when he was sent home, where he too, started coughing up blood. We had some things in common—a shitty kind of shared history, but maybe those are the best kinds.

"Mind your own God-damned business. Don't you have some shoes to shine? And I'm not your 'Lieutenant', spook," I said.

"And thank the Lord for that. The last person I'd want leading me into any kind of battle is a crazy, red-neck cracker suffering from bad dreams like a kindergartener with a wet diaper. And the only spooks around here are the poor souls from the A ward," Sinclair said waving a fist like an Eightball in my face.

"Hey, I'm just calling a spade a spade."

"Of all the bunks in this sanatorium, I got the one next to the cornbread, cracker asshole."

"It could be worse. You could be next to Old Man McGee. I heard he *really is* a Negro hater. Whereas I'm a Negro debater."

We both grinned and bit the laughter down. Laughter or shooting the shit too much caused coughing fits. Coughing fits were never a good thing. If you coughed long enough and hard enough, something was bound to come out that shouldn't have. Hemorrhages, the signature of tuberculosis and the stamp on the death warrant, in some cases. I threw an *Esquire Magazine* at him. Sinclair went to reading it without saying another word, moving a toothpick in his mouth from one side to the other.

I WAS IN the B Ward of the Barlow Tuberculosis Sanatorium in Los Angeles, California. The building was a foreboding, red-bricked fortress with Spanish-styled, white-painted arches that led long and wide outside the entrance. Barlow's had always been a consumption sanatorium since being first built in 1901. It was up in the hills, on the outskirts of the city, next to a large park and the baseball stadium. On the weekends, we could hear the crowds cheering for their teams. A strange sound that echoed off the hills and the emptiness between the city and the sanatorium, creating an eerie space in the distance between.

The sanatorium was cool all year round and comfortable enough. Boredom seemed to be more of a problem than the consumption itself. Staff and patients alike pretty much kept to themselves or the small cliques they'd formed over coughs, time, and card games.

I had been there since early April 1949—six months in. Being in the B Ward meant doctors had given you the okay for one hour of recreation a day and a bath. That really meant one hour to sit in a chair in the garden, or in a chair in the cafeteria, or in a chair by the French windows. One hour only and a whole lot of sitting around. When I wasn't sitting, I spent the other twenty-three hours lying prostrate, napping, catching up on my reading, listening to the radio, talking in whispers, and trying not to cough up my lungs. Spending twenty-three hours a day like that and shuffling from one chair to another to sit down, felt like some kind of a small victory.

I was in the same situation as every other poor son of a bitch on B Ward. It could have been worse. I could have been back in the A Ward with twenty-four hours bed rest—with doctors itching to remove my ribs and forcibly collapse a lung every other day. It seemed excessive to have a lung pierced by a long needle-like straw being slid through the ribs and pumped with nitrogen until the lung crumpled up like a used, paper bag. "That's what the Japs call karma," I'd always thought as I felt the doctors slide the needle into my lung.

The Doc kept saying my health and luck were improving. He gave me good odds of getting out of the sanatorium in a month or so. He said I should stay hopeful. I reminded him that every nag he gambled on lost. He pretended to laugh, and I pretended to be hopeful.

IT WAS A Wednesday afternoon in October. B Ward had just eaten lunch—the place smelled like meatloaf and gravy. The green-tiled floor shone like turquoise water as the light filtered through the windows. The summer had died slowly, and it was still warm outside. Frankie Laine's *That Lucky Old Sun* playing on the radio. The nurses always had the volume good and loud to drown out the constant droning of coughs. Loud, the way I preferred it. The song carried a good tune that had me tapping my foot to the beat. It brought back a mix of memories from a late, Friday afternoon in June. Frankie's hit blaring out into the ward as Jean and I snuck into The Doc's office to make quick-but-unhurried love on his desk. The bribe for the use of his office had cost me a hefty chunk of change, but The Doc was a degenerate gambler who had his patients' mental and physical wellbeing in the forefront of his mind and some hefty gambling debts and flings with some of the younger nurses, that he thought no one knew about, concealed at the backside of his mind. The Doc was older than me by a few years (middle thirties), athletic, and the son of German immigrants I'd guessed, with his hard intonations and kraut family name. It takes a thief to catch a thief and you can't bullshit a bullshitter, being an immigrant myself.

TWENTY YEARS EARLIER, in 1929, I had come over to The States on a ship from Belfast, Ireland, with my folks and younger sister. I was ten years old—one month before the Wall Street Crash. It hadn't been a good time to arrive in America, looking for a better life. There wasn't one.

My father always wore a faded-blue corduroy jacket, a cracked, red face, and a rolled cigarette at the corner of his grim mouth. He shouted or laughed a lot and called me 'Boy'. I don't think I ever heard him call me by my given name, Seamus. A name I'd changed to 'Scott' as soon as I'd finally started school in California. Hard enough being an Irish immigrant in The Depression, let alone having an accent and a real bog-trotters name like Seamus Kelly. My father had finally got a job as a builder's laborer then quickly fell back into the bottom of a bottle. My mother, a beautiful-yet-worn woman, stayed in the kitchen and prayed the rosary. I grew up poor in America, because we were Irish immigrants in The Depression—a family of clichés who never stood a fucking chance.

In a country populated by immigrants, it was difficult to be a foreigner. The newly arrived foreigners clustered together, sticking to what they knew and weary of what they didn't. The Italians, the Jews, the Orientals all had their own stores, streets, gangs, and little strongholds. There were two types of Irish. The Irish who'd already been in the United States a couple of generations, who were already integrated into the system, and the newly arrived, fresh off the boat Irish. Neither group was fond of the other. All the immigrants newly arrived in The United States had one thing in common: they were all scrambling hard to make it in a place where they'd been told that the streets were paved with gold. The streets weren't paved with gold, they were littered with shit, trash and the dispossessed. It was tough and you had to get tough to make it.

I was targeted early because I was a fresh off the boat, scrawny kid with no friends and no roots. I tried to lose my accent and talk like a Californian to stop the neighborhood kids beating the shit out of me, but the accent didn't take. I learnt it was easier and more beneficial to learn to box. When they knew you could fight and you could hurt them too, the neighborhood kids always moved on to someone else, some other kid that was fresh off a boat and wet behind the ears. I'd never been much good at boxing though. I'd start off well, cut off the ring, land a lot of heavy shots—but as soon as I got into the deep waters, I'd lose focus, drop my guard, get shook, freeze and finally lose heart. Half punch-drunk before I'd started shaving. My start in the United States of America. Irish, poor, and beaten. Poor, Irish and fighting. As good an education as any.

ONE NIGHT, THREE years after the crash, my father stumbled in front of a streetcar. He died slow and bad in a charity ward. I went to see him there. In that place that smelt of stale piss and stale medicine. He had looked very small and fragile and not like my father at all. The room full of retching and gibbering wrecks of people dying the way they'd lived. My father one of them. He had squeezed my hand; the first and the last warm body contact we'd ever had. I sat next to his cot wishing I were anywhere else but there in that room and then he'd died. One moment he was my father and the next a shell in an overcrowded, noisy room. He went from being something to being nothing instantaneously. I'd never really known him. In death he had helped our family more than he had ever done in life. Our mother received compensation from the Streetcar Company, and she saved it all, so my sister and I could go to college and get educated to better ourselves.

My constantly suffering mother. She died of a heart attack seven years after my father, one year after my daughter was born, three months after Pearl Harbor and seven days after I signed up with the Marines to fight in the war.

My parents had worked all their lives and had nothing to show for it after they died. Not a pot to piss in. They had spent their lives working, but for nothing. They should have stayed back in Kerry.

THE DOC. HE didn't have any of those kinds of problems, though. He'd come from old money and he appeared to be untouched by doubt, worry or insecurity, or even a shitty childhood, which most people had, rich or poor. The Doc was one of life's lucky, unblemished ones. His blonde hair always carefully combed; his clothes always immaculately cleaned. He had the kind of classically blue-eyed handsome face that could have run for president one day and the perfectly practiced smile to go with it.

"No kissing or swapping saliva mind, eh, Sport? You could possibly still be contagious. And please don't make too much of a mess of my office, you old dog," The Doc had said as he snatched the roll of bills from my hand, one of many I'd smuggled in with me because no matter where you end up in life, there's always someone waiting to be bought off. He'd winked and given me the knowing elbow of a man who told his wife he was working late while he took advantage of a young nurse in his black Cadillac. He thought we had camaraderie. He was wrong. I needed to pay him off and shine him on to get what I wanted, like I did with most people. What I had wanted and needed most was time alone with Jean in a private place—his office.

That day in The Doc's office was the second occasion Jean had been able to visit me at the sanatorium. She had spent the visiting hour weeping when she saw me the first time.

"Oh my God, Scotty!" she'd cried, her hand on my face. "You look like a skeleton; you've lost so much weight! Aren't they feeding you here at all? I'm going to speak to the doctors and give them a piece of my mind. They're practically starving you here."

I had reassured her, of course. When you're stuck in a state sanatorium there wasn't much else to do but reassure people. She had sat uncomfortably by my bedside, telling me excitedly about Hollywood, explaining the ins and outs of the work she was getting as an extra—movie-star gossip. She'd ranted about her selfish, abusive ex-husband, Dexter, and his new, soon-to-be wife. She had chatted about her daughter who was a few years younger than my own and about her daily life in general. I sat propped up in bed, listened, and nodded my head reassuringly. She would cry into a white, wadded-up handkerchief in her small hand every time I coughed up blood—an unfulfilling and awkward visit for both of us.

The second time she'd arrived for the visiting hour, I'd quickly taken her hand and led her to The Doc's office. My heart thumping in my itchy chest, trying my best not to have a coughing fit and spoil these well-oiled, slightly expensive plans. Old Man McGee stared at us from his bunk by the door with eyes that bulged out of his head, slack jawed and envious.

"Are you sure The Doctor said this was okay, Scotty?" she asked as I opened the door to the office and guided her in with my arm around her waist. I nodded and winked. Jean had stood in the doorway admiring the place.

"Oh, wow! Gosh. What a beautiful room. That desk must be an antique. It's like a set on a movie, isn't it? The office of a big shot. It's such a beautiful office. Your doctor has such elegant taste," she had said as she stepped out of her red, high heels and rolled down her silk stockings. She didn't want them to get ruined, she'd whispered self-consciously with a crooked smile. I locked the door, leaving the key in the hole, and pushed her up onto the desk. Jean wiggled her hips to get herself into a comfortable, ready position.

"Jean, you're only mine. You know that, right?" I had asked as I slid inside her as effortlessly as always. Our bodies attuned to each other with experience and compatibility. She had untied her long, light brown hair and unbuttoned her red blouse. She hitched up her black skirt further, her legs up higher around my waist and murmured, "I've always been the one who loves you most. I love you most of all. I'm here with you now. I'm the one with you in this place. Where's she? Your ex-wife isn't here, is she? Or those tramps from the bar? I'm the one who loves you the most. I love you most of all. It's me. It's me, Scotty. Say it to me. Say it to me, please, Scotty."

I said it. Repeated it with each thrust. She turned her face away and put it over my shoulder, away from my erratic heavy breathing. I felt her breasts wet with perspiration against my chest and tasted the Chanel Number Five on the flesh of her throat and neck. Her breathing whispered in my ear. Her hair softly against my face. She held me close. Gripped at my hip and neck attempting to control the momentum and force. As I came closer, she told me what she'd always told me,

"Not inside, Scotty, huh? Not inside."

I thrust the last and I finished inside her. I couldn't help it. Though I didn't regret it. I had thought it was crazy, but it was as though I wanted a piece of me to leave that place with her. I wanted a part of me to remain inside her. Stay with her on the bus ride home. Escape with her. Stay a part of her until she showered me away down into the darkness of the drain.

She immediately pushed me off and away from her. Let herself down from the edge of the desk, knocking over a tray of paper clips, a desk calendar and a silver picture frame of The Doc and his family.

"Jesus Christ, Scott. I can't believe you just did that to me again. You know what that puts me through each and every time. The worry. The fear. The dreadful thoughts… Waiting for the blood to come. It's me that has to deal with it, not you. If I got in the motherly way, I could just kiss my Hollywood career goodbye. I've already tried being a housewife and it wasn't the most compatible for me and you know that. Jesus! I already have one daughter and a divorce. I don't need any more problems like that. I've been trying so hard and now I'm finally getting parts in the movies... Scotty? Scotty, are you listening to me?"

"I'm listening," I said, wiping myself off with a tissue from a box of Kleenex on The Doc's desk.

She pulled on her black lace panties and then buttoned her

blouse as she spoke.

"My friend Robert. You know the actor Robert Cummings? Well, he thinks I've got what it takes to make it to the top. I'm meeting so many important people, Scotty. I met the actor Kirk Douglas on the set of my newest film. He showed me around the whole of the studio. He's such a nice man. And so popular, everyone kept coming up to us to shake his hand and say hello. Do you know of him?"

"No, I don't."

"Well, we are in a movie together, it's called 'Young Man with a Horn'. I got to wear a long beautiful green dress on the set for my role. I looked just like a European princess. I'm just starting to fix my life properly, you know? I'm finally making it, Scotty. Finally. You can be such a selfish bastard sometimes. I bet you're not even the slightest bit sorry about it, are you now?"

She was steadily rolling on her stockings and glaring at me with those piercing eyes. The lightest blue and cool with something behind the shine and shade of the irises that seemed to always linger there waiting for something from me. Waiting for what? I didn't know. That old gut feeling settled in then at the bottom of my stomach. That rabid, old bloodhound. That sinking realization, I got sometimes about somethings.

"Are you fucking him?"

"Am I what?" she pouted.

"Are you fucking him?" I crossed my arms. Dropped them to my sides and then crossed them again.

"What are you talking about now?" she giggled, a little too high pitched.

We had played this scene out more than a few times and we both knew our lines by heart and acted it out for an audience of two.

"I asked, Jean, are you fucking him?"

"Am I fucking who, Scott?"

"The actor guy? Your good pal, your best friend?"

"Robert Cummings?"

"Yeah. Him. Are you?"

"Oh, Jesus Christ, Scott! Are you really going to start this again?!"

"Just answer the question, Jean. Are you fucking him? *Yes or no?*"

"This is ridiculous, Scott. You're being ridiculous. And, for your information, he is married. He's married to a wonderful woman. You're always so suspicious. Always jealous. It's really quite unattractive, you know?"

"What about the other actor, that Kirk guy? The guy who gave you the fucking studio tour?"

"Jesus, Scott! How can you even ask me questions like that? You've got some nerve! What kind of a woman do you think I am? Is that what you think of me? That I'm just some tramp who goes for any old guy? Is that what you think of me?"

"That doesn't answer the question though does it, Jean? Stop evading the question, Jean."

"You're really crazy! You know that? You're fucking crazy, Scott! You should be in a mental asylum, not a sanatorium like this place! I came all the way out here to see you and you treat me like this? I'm really upset, Scott. How can you treat me this way? You've ruined my day completely."

"Just answer the question, Jean. You still haven't answered it. Just answer the *fucking question.*"

"What if I don't? Are you going to hit me again like last time, on Christmas Day? Are you? You gave me two black eyes! Lieutenant Scott, the war hero, *the tough guy!*"

"Jesus, Jean. I've said sorry for that day a thousand times already."

"That's your way to solve all your problems though, isn't it? With your *fists*… or a gun."

"What are you talking about now? The war?"

"People gossip a lot in Hollywood, Scott. I know people. I've met people. Important people. They know all about you and they told me all about it. All your filthy, dirty, little secrets."

"What are you talking about?"

"I always thought it strange, a man back from the war, no job, living in a beautiful house like yours and then buying that bar on Fairfax. Now, I know how you could afford all those things and live like that!"

"What're you talking about woman? Who have you been talking to? Who told you and what did they tell you?"

"I know all about you, Scott! You pretend to be so high and mighty, but you're worse than any of us. You're the *worst*."

"Oh yeah? Then why don't you enlighten me, Jean?"

"You killed people, Scott. I heard the rumors. You and the mob and all that other jazz. Scott Kelly, the crazy Irish Marine, who hurt people for Bugsy Siegel and other mobsters. I should have known it the first night that I laid eyes on you, the people you were with. Your life, well, it could be a Hollywood movie script, couldn't it? Scott Kelly, the cold-hearted killer, right? Don't you think? Scott Kelly who shoots whole families dead. Scott Kelly who killed a lit—"

I slapped her across the cheek with the back of my hand. Not hard, just one of those stunning kinds of jabs. Just enough to stop her from talking anymore. She was being hysterical. More of a reflex than anything else.

She didn't even step back though, she just glared at me with those big blue eyes, jutting her chin into the air, daring me to try it again.

I looked at her. I didn't know what to say. I tied my robe. Loosened it and then tied it again. She was so perfectly stunning and righteous at that moment that all I could do was stare.

CHAPTER 2

SOMETHING INSIDE ME was stuck after I came back from the war—discharged early at the ass end of 1945. Stuck like a rusty cog in an old wristwatch. I wasn't ticking away like everyone else anymore. I didn't know much about anything then, but I knew that much. I couldn't feel things the same way other people could. It was like a faucet that went from rushed water to a slow drip.

My wife, Beth, and our daughter had noticed real quick. I wasn't the same kid who'd graduated from Stanford University with a degree in English Literature. No longer the happy husband nor the doting father—a very different animal altogether. My wife and daughter had grown cold and guarded, as a result of my behavior. They became careful around me, like I was a landmine waiting to go off and tear into limbs. It was a kind of self-preservation for them, I'd guessed later.

The only emotion that appeared to still work within me was anger and it was a deep rage that seemed to spurt out at random times of the day, triggered by random events, a broken shoelace, a spilt glass of water, an overcooked steak. A disease I had brought back within me from tropical climates in the Pacific. A tumor always spreading inside me and leaking bile all over my life. I'd suddenly explode during dinner over the table or while making coffee in the morning, snarling, and growling at my family. They stared at me like small, scared things unable to move or look away.

I started drunken fights with anyone whose face I deemed offensive enough, went to cheap motels to fuck the kind of women who chewed gum when they talked and drank alone and heavy in dive bars. Anything to get the slightest bit of feeling back. But the more I tried to get some kind of emotion back, the emptier I felt and the angrier I seemed to become.

There are only so many times you can slip the wedding ring off your finger and pocket it before all meaning is lost. What used to be your life starts falling apart at the seams. The chasm that had been torn between my wife and me grew longer and deeper. Beth struggled on, like any good wife, trying her best to understand me—be supportive—but it was March 1947, after nearly eight years of marriage, that she finally filed for divorce. We had married before I graduated college—her pregnancy hastened the union. We'd tried our best in the beginning—we did love each other very much—but a lot of things had changed after the war. She was tired of picking up broken glass, finding lipstick and blood stains on my shirts, and trying to hide from guests and visiting relatives the holes I'd punched in the walls. I wasn't surprised; I didn't blame her. I signed the divorce papers the morning I received them in the mail. I sat at our dining-room table—the same place my daughter had splashed gravy on us, done her homework, and eaten the birthday cakes her always-suffering mother had baked—and signed the yellow legal forms on the dotted line. No, I didn't blame her. I signed and sent them back to her sister's address in Brooklyn, New York City, where she'd been living since she left me. I didn't feel much about anything as I put the papers in the mailbox—no sadness, no disappointment, no feelings of regret.

It was only a little while later that I lay in bed, flipping through an old novel, when a Christmas card had fallen out. I had recalled the inscription by looking at the cream envelope in my hand, but I opened it anyway and read the intricate cursive inside:

> To My Dearest Scott,
> Thank you so much for taking me to New York for Christmas. I had a wonderful time, and my family really adored you. Standing at the top of the Empire State with you was the best feeling in my life. I really adore you and love you so much.
> You're an amazing husband, and I know you're going to be a

perfect father. I know we are going to have a happy family and life together until we grow old.
Love Always, Your Bethy.

It was only after reading the aged card that I finally noticed how much I had truly lost—how much had deserted me. I realized that it was all gone—everything—and I couldn't ever get it back again. "They're better without me," I'd told myself. I had only caused my daughter harm. She was better far away from the broken shards of her father. I felt a twist of regret as I placed the card back into the book. Still, there was no sadness, no heartbreak, no real feelings at all. Just a lingering numbness somewhere inside. A gnawing emptiness.

ONE NIGHT I sat at the dining table until the early hours of the morning, listening to the sounds of the emptiness. I realized that I had survived the war only by returning as a ghost. A deal I'd made with the devil. A ghost that haunted my own home. I'd bought the place in the Wilshire district of L.A. It was a beautiful four-bedroom Tudor style place, that I'd bought for my family after I'd gotten better-paying work and moved us out of the shitty little apartment we had lived in the months after I got back to the States. After my wife and daughter left, I walked from room to empty room, drinking from a bottle and punching more holes in the walls. It was a family house without a family. A family home that I was alone in. A silent house, empty of family conversations and void of family smells. I tried to stay there as little as possible.

I SPENT A lot of time in the bars and clubs around Los Angeles (uptown and downtown), drinking with the important friends who had given me jobs that paid a lot of dough for similar things I had done for free in the war. I shacked up with showgirls and bargirls nightly, to attempt to fill the void that had swallowed my life—always hungover the next morning and a little more numb than the day before.

A club was where I'd first met Jean. Florentine Gardens—a sleazy, little dive in Hollywood, all but on the verge of bankruptcy. It was early 1947, and Jean was working there as a dancer. We were introduced to each other by the owner, Hansen—an oily, little man who liked to connect young girls with important people to try and ingratiate himself into their circles. The guy was half a fucking pimp. I didn't consider myself an important person, but I was sitting at a table, drinking with Benjamin Siegel and Anthony Cornero—two of the most important people in Los Angeles at the time, who I'd worked for since I'd got back.

I was taken with Jean as soon as I saw her. She was beautiful, but it was a tainted kind of beauty—a broken elegance. I sat across from her, watching the lights dancing in her eyes, the way she would smile quickly then look around self-consciously. Déjà vu. It felt as though I already knew her—the taste of her lips, her hair over my face. I'd taken Jean home that very night. We'd taken a taxicab to my place and we barely got in the front door before she had gone to her knees, unbuckled my belt, eased down my jockey shorts, and taken me in her warm, wet mouth. She knew exactly what to do. Women like her always did and I liked women like her best of all. We were like high-school kids on the stairs, in the bedroom, and again in the morning. That first-time, rushed, impatient, fumbled, nice-to-meet-you kind of fuck.

I realized afterwards that Jean was very different from other women; she didn't seem bitter and used up after spreading her legs. She was mischievous in conversation and sex. She made me laugh. Genuinely laugh. After that first night, I had tried to see her every moment that I could get the time with her. She really started to fill the void that I felt in my life with my wife and daughter gone. It wasn't a temporary nightly fix like the other girls had been. As crazy as it sounds, there was something about her that made me feel almost superhuman. I was the funniest guy in the room, the best lover, the most handsome, the most intelligent, the strongest. Everything I did made her feel good. I was her hero, her priest, her teacher, her father and her lover and I needed and wanted to be all those things for her.

She needed me and I needed her.

And things between us went along like that for nearly a year until Christmas Day, 1947 and then she was gone. She left me out as soon as she had taken me in.

WITH MY FAMILY gone and then Jean gone, I couldn't stand the house another week and sold it soon after. Cashed everything in and cashed everything out and with some of the other dough I had owed to me here and there, I bought a bar with a small apartment for living on the second floor. If I was going to be drinking every day, I might as well do it in my own place. I made it into an Irish Bar. An Irish bar in a Jewish neighborhood. I never had been good at making business decisions. The bar had my family's name proudly above the door, 'KELLY'S BAR' in large gold font with a green neon lit Shamrock that burned out about the same time I started coughing up mouthfuls of the red stuff. Even at that time, looking at the crimson smears on my hands, wiping the blood from my mouth, I still felt nothing. Nothing except for Jean.

It was always Jean. She had smoothed over the broken shards and had taken the sharp edges off of everything better than a bottle ever could. My remedy, my cure. It was Jean who had dragged me to the doctors. Jean who had been with me for the X-rays. Jean who had been there with me, crying and tearing a piece of tissue into confetti as I finally got my results, tuberculosis in the left lung and the sanatorium for 5 to 8 months. And finally, Jean who had been waving goodbye to me, telling me she'd visit me as soon as the doctors said she was allowed to. Jean. Yeah, it was always Jean.

The only problem I'd ever had was with her incessant neediness. Jean was the type of woman who always needed someone. She always needed to be wanted, to be adored, loved. She always had one guy coming in the front door, as one was leaving out the back. A constant conveyer belt of shoe salesmen, movie producers, sailors, bank clerks and Hollywood stars. She couldn't stand to be alone, because, I had guessed, she couldn't really stand to be with herself. The longer she was alone, the longer she would have to spend with herself as company. Misery loves company. I lost count of the times I found another man's razor in her bathroom, a necktie in her bedroom or found her sat in some bar, smiling across from some little prick who was just going to fuck her and dispose of her after. I would have to tell them to beat it, quick. Jean loved to watch men fight for her. It drove me crazy because I wanted her for myself. I didn't want to share her with anyone else. Jean and I had fought over these things tirelessly. She always argued I had the wrong idea, that I was too suspicious, too jealous, the men just friends. I was trying to tie her down and she didn't like that. She was always saying she wanted to be free.

I'd tried to change her and show her that we only needed each other. I thought she had understood. I'd tried to give her all the attention, love, and adoration she'd needed, but it was never enough for her. Never sufficient. In the end, most of all, it was her lies to me that stung the worst. She could look me directly in the face with those big blue eyes of hers and lie like it was the easiest thing in the world. Her being an actress— maybe it was that.

SHE HAD LEFT The Doc's office in the sanatorium quickly that day, after the fight, and said she'd see me again later. She didn't say anything else. She didn't say she loved me. She quietly closed the door behind her and just like that, she was gone again. I listened to the sound of her high heels as she walked down the green tiled floor to the front entrance, thinking to myself that the women who are the best at walking away are always the ones who you need the most. I went and sat behind The Doc's desk. I looked at his family's photo in the silver frame that I had put back to where it was placed before Jean had knocked it down on the floor. The Doc had it so his patients could look it over admiringly while they were sat across from him getting bad news. Two little boys with gap-toothed grins and a wife that looked happy she'd married a successful doctor and not a dentist. That all American, Stars and Stripes kind of family, the kind you're likely to see in catalogues or magazine advertisements selling toothpaste and summer homes.

I wondered where my family was at that moment. I contemplated what my daughter was doing and if she thought about me at all. The absent father. I missed her. It was a rotten wound that wouldn't heal in my chest the whole time. I had realized too late that she was the one person in my life who probably loved me because that was all she knew how to do. There was no ulterior motive in her love for me. I missed her. But, every time I had looked at my daughters face before she left with her mother, I'd seen a little girl who was unsure of how to act around me, slow and careful in her movements, always watchful and wide eyed. Seeing *that* in her was worse than not seeing her at all.

I thought about Jean going back to Hollywood to flirt with her actor friends, producers and God knew who else. I looked out of The Doc's large window and saw him talking with her in the parking lot. He was showing her his Cadillac. I had to admit it was a beautiful automobile. Jean was admiring the hood mascot, a chrome woman shaped like a bayonet that glistened in the sun. The sky coming on orange and red and their shadows pointing like fingers towards me. Jean kept giggling and primping her hair. The Doc raising the toe of his shoe on its heel and pointing it at her, grinning. The little prick actually gave her his business card and put his hand on her shoulder as they talked. They stood laughing together. Jean twisting her hips. The Doc then leaning on the bonnet of his flash ride. I growled. My right eye ached. I started coughing and hacked blood onto his mahogany desk. I contemplated wiping it off with the sleeve of my robe but decided to leave it there pooled before his family's photograph. When I looked out again Jean saw me. She waved half-heartedly. I didn't wave back. I went back to my bunk to lie down for another twenty-three hours.

FRANKIE LAINE'S *That Lucky Old Sun* finished playing and one of the nurses switched the radio off. I got up slowly and shuffled outside. Head still aching with remnants of the dreams. That last time with Jean, that Friday afternoon in June, the day of the fight had been nearly four months before, and I hadn't seen or heard from her since. Not another visit, not a telephone call, nor a letter or a postcard. Nothing. I didn't know what to think of it, but I thought about her every single day. We had gone a long time without any communication the last few times we had fought, and she'd left, especially after what had happened on Christmas Day of '47. She always needed time and I was good at giving her that. A pro at waiting for her and I was still waiting for her to arrive, smiling, and calling my name when I saw Sinclair shuffling over the lawn to me waving a newspaper. It was after lunch, recreation hour. I was sat in the shade, underneath a stunted palm tree in the garden, trying to read an old copy of *Esquire Magazine* and I knew something wasn't right by the way he fumbled with the pages of the newspaper and avoided looking at my face.

"Say, looky here Lieutenant, is this the girl who came to see you a few months back in June? The beauty? Is this your girl?" he whispered wheezily when he came close enough to talk to me.

I took that day's edition of the *Los Angeles Examiner* from his trembling coffee skinned hand and immediately saw Jean's face. Her face next to the image of the girl they found all hacked up in 1947. Jean's picture directly next to the Black Dahlia girls' picture. Fuck. I read the headline.

'GLAMOUR GIRL GONE'

I tried to read the words underneath the headline, but my eyes kept flashing back to her photograph. I felt my skin burning.

Jean was smiling at the camera lens, her eyes looked into mine. Her brow and smile strained. Wearing her long chestnut hair tied up with a large ribbon trailing down past her breasts and a sort of charcoal negligee that showed off her cleavage. A teasing hand on her hip as though daring the photographer to make a pass at her. Jean, the one who said she loved me the most. The coughing started small, the way it always did. Ripping up my chest like a deformed chuckle or a rabid dog's growl, building itself up and rupturing my body. I fell to the ground on my knees, coughing and convulsing, specks of blood splattered her beautiful face and the headline with pinkish-red ink spots.

'GLAMOUR GIRL GONE'
'GONE'

I could hear Sinclair shouting, concerned voices all around me, shuffling feet and felt hands grabbing at my body, trying to lift me, but I wasn't there. It was as though I was underwater, drowning again in darkness.

I was submerged. Jean was leaping from the cliff. She screamed for me to help her. Help. Her.

I tried to swim.

Waltzing Matilda hummed by a child.

Jean was falling again, my daughter in her arms. My daughter screamed *Daddy!*

My boots were too heavy, sucked by mud.

I saw my Thompson machine gun slowly fall away into a patch of yellow grass.

I tried to reach the surface. My chest burning from sea water and Jean screaming, but my chest hurt so much, I was too weak.

The little girl screamed "*Daddy!*"

Waltzing Matilda…

Everything faded to black. The darkness consumed me. It always did and then I was on the beaches again.

STEPPING ONTO THE dust of Okinawa. An atmosphere of intruding into a haunted house, the mouth of a fanged beast. The air was heavy, the humidity crawled over our skin, grew stale and festered there like lice. We scratched at our flesh and listened to the sounds of the island breathing.

The birds sang so slowly. Insects whined and droned. A huge bat wrapped in black shroud-like wings hung from a tree, a dark eyed monster watching us.

Aliens.

Outsiders.

We walked through bamboo forests, deserted villages, jungles, and paddy fields.

Ghosts.

In the morning light, smoke and mist hung over the ground, distorting and fading the colors from things.

Limbo.

Mosquitos feasted on our flesh until they were too bloated to fly. The afternoon sun relentless upon us. A fever.

Deeper inland we set up base at the bottom of a ridge and scraped our way into the rocky ground, to burrow in. Set up trip flares around our perimeter, barbed wire, machine gun nests. Tried to sleep between minutes. Flicked fire ants from our sweat dampened, soiled uniforms. I wanted to go home.

HOME...

MY MOTHER HAD said that it wasn't a war for a Kerry boy. I'd wanted to explain to her that once college was finished with and after Pearl Harbor, there were no excuses left not to go. Not to sign up appeared weak. Cowardly. Spineless. Yellow. People looked at you strange if you weren't in a uniform back home; something was wrong with you. You were less of a man. The only thing left to do was sign up. Enlist. There hadn't been much of a choice. Peer pressure was a bitch in high heels and a college sweater. I'd wanted to explain that to her, but I didn't. I'd said some bullshit about duty and patriotism. I'd lied to her and she'd died a little while after. I found her slumped dead in the kitchen wearing a blue cotton dress, clutching her rosary and a knife in her hands. She'd been peeling potatoes. Slumped in a puddle of piss and peelings, dead, but for the first time her face looked finally at ease, relaxed and I could see the beautiful young girl she'd once been. The girl my father had married in the village church back in Kerry. The woman who had stood by my father through all the drinking, all the screaming, yelling and all the bullshit that went with it. I buried her next to him on a sunny Wednesday afternoon, biting my lower lip over the muddy hole in the ground, my infant daughter sleeping in her mother's arms. People who had known my parents muttered their sympathies and shook my hand as I stared into the darkness of the grave.

Darkness...

DARKNESS CAME SO slowly; the island came alive around us. We eyeballed the thick green foliage of the tree lines. I clutched my Thompson and trembled, shivered and scratched. I had sent out two of the Marines from my platoon to secure a listening post at the edge of the ridge; they'd not checked in.

The sky full of stars and the Milky Way the clearest I'd ever seen it. It should have been beautiful, but it wasn't. Okinawa should have been beautiful, but it wasn't. The atmosphere put its sweaty, damp weight everywhere, soiling and rotting all it touched. I eyeballed the suffocating greenery and waited.

A little after midnight, a yellow moon screaming in the night sky, the trip flares illuminated the darkness of the land in front of us into a smoky haze of light and shadows. We saw them then, the Japs. They were running towards our camp, sprinting, rolling, tumbling down the ridge. An avalanche of screaming limbs. A dark horde of bodies clambering over rocks, through trees towards us, wailing and yelling unearthly sounds. That terrifying scream of '*BANZAI*'. Banzai, the Japanese way of saying 'sink or swim'.

SINK OR SWIM. When you've been backed up to the ropes, your arms burn and feel like they're full of boiling water. You've taken a straight-right to the face that explodes like an electric bomb blast through your nervous system and you've taken a body shot to the gut that ripped all of the air out of your lungs. The crowd jeering through cigar smoke and beer breath. Sink or swim. Sink or fucking swim. It was always at those times when those words echoed through my skull. The roar of the drunken audience faded and only the sounds of my father's words and my own choking heartbeat remained. Sink or swim.

He had said those words to me when I was seven years old, stood at the end of a small rotten pier at Inch beach in Kerry.

"You're going to learn to swim today, Boy. It's about time you learnt. Today's your first lesson, and it's the most important lesson of them all."

I'd stripped off to my pants and stood shivering in the late afternoon orange, red sky. My skinny arms around myself. Staring at the hills that surrounded the beach like crocodiles. Wanting to go home.

"It's sink or swim, Boy. Are you ready?"

I didn't understand, but I'd nodded.

"It's sink or fucking swim now." My father scooped me up swiftly into his arms and then hurled me from the pier into the gray sea beneath. The shock of the impact and the freezing water knocked the air out of me. Saltwater burnt through my nostrils and stung my throat. I couldn't breathe. All I could hear was my heartbeat, the rolling of the waves and my father shouting,

"Sink or swim, Boy! Sink or fucking swim."

Those words would always jostle their way through the crowd and climb into the ring with me when I was fighting in the smokers' as a teenager and I'd always do what I did the day my father threw me from the pier. I'd sink. I'd swallow the punches like seawater and drown. Wait for my father or the referee to jump in and pull me out from the darkness. I'd never had the heart. When the devil came to stare me down, I always looked away first. And all the times I'd hit the canvas and all the times I didn't have the heart followed me across the world, onto the beaches of Okinawa. Sink or swim.

Sink or fucking swim…

EXPLOSIONS JOLTED THROUGH my body. I didn't give the order, frozen again in the shadow of my own empty courage, but tracer rounds, bursts of bullets, machine guns and rifles blazed open the night. The twilight ripped open by muzzle flashes of rifles and machine guns. I aimed my Thompson into the night sky above the mass and fired into nothingness. Too weak. I had no heart. I was a failure as a boxer, a failure as a lieutenant and a failure as a Marine. I didn't have the heart to kill. Tears disfigured my face and I fired into the black sky through blurry, wet vision like a cowardly fool. Watched the bullets from my platoon tear the Japs into pieces until nothing was left but dark smoking piles of things that were once human beings. The smell of gunpowder and smoke was cloying in the night air. I counted up to ten. I counted myself out—waiting for the sound of a bell that I knew would never ring.

After the gloom of night, in the light of the day, the morning sun painted the corpses of more than forty Okinawan civilians orange and red. The Japs had used them as a human shield to try and escape, a sacrificial getaway. The Marines sat down amongst the pulpy thick mess of bloody women, children and elderly and ate breakfast from their C Rations, covering the cans of meat and gravy with their palms to stop the swarms of flies from crawling into their food as well. I smoked cigarette after cigarette to try and mask the scent that radiated from the dead like a noxious gas. Shit, blood, and meat. glancing everywhere but at the soup of faces, rags, and limbs.

Later, after an hour of searching, we finally found the Marines I'd sent to establish a listening post by the ridge, both naked in a rocky crevice. The Japs had butchered them. Sliced off their arms and legs and left them to bleed out with their cocks in their cringing mouths. The bloody stumps of their arms and legs congealed and swarming with insects.

I felt something inside me slow down and then stop. Just stop. I'd wiped the vomit from my mouth, stared down at the two kids. I didn't know what to say to them. They were dead. I'd sent them to deaths as ridiculous, cruel, and humiliating as that. A failure as a lieutenant. How could I lead men out of this war when I was barely surviving it myself? I couldn't sink any further than I had already. The devil came to look me in the eye and winked. I stared back.

My mother had been right, this war was no place for a Kerry boy and the Kerry boy wouldn't survive it. He was already dead.

Sink or swim...

MY MOTHER SAT on the steps of our house in California as I ran into her arms with wet eyes. The neighborhood kids had beaten me bloody again. Ten years old.

Sink or swim...

Then I was a teenager, an amateur boxer in the smokers.

Sink or swim...

A husband. A father.

Sink or swim...

Then a Marine, a second lieutenant.

Sink or swim...

My mother took me in her arms and held me there. I was safe there. The stench of potato peels and urine bloated my lungs and I realized I was in the embrace of a corpse. Somewhere a baby wailed, something inside me had stopped and Jean was gone. I needed to find her.

Sink or fucking swim.

CHAPTER 3

THE FOLLOWING MORNING, after the news of Jean's disappearance, I sat across from The Doc, looking around his office. Thick, leather-bound books filled dark mahogany bookshelves. Old medical diagrams were framed on the ivory colored, oriental wallpaper. An examination table, newly cleaned and perfectly white on the other side of the office with a blue separation curtain around it. A large wooden model of The Doc's yacht on the windowsill. The Doc even had his own private door that led out into the parking lot and grounds. He didn't have to enter through the front entrance like the lower classes he probably secretly detested. The desk calendar read "*Oct 13, '49*".

Jean had gone missing on the 7th of October, according to the newspapers. She'd been gone for six days. Six whole days without any clues or leads to where she might have been. I could almost feel her in the room. Smell her perfume there. Taste her there. Getting out of the God-damned sanatorium and finding her was all that mattered to me. She needed me. I knew I needed to find her. The newspaper had printed words such as '*gone*', '*missing*', and '*disappeared*', but there was no evidence of violence, no body, and no suspicious suspects. Jean was still out there somewhere. Why she had decided to disappear, I didn't know, but I was going to find her. Help her.

"You know, I'm really sorry Mr. Kelly," The Doc said.

"Call me Scott, please, Doc."

"Uh, okay, yes, you're quite right. Scott. Well, anyhow, Scott, as I was saying, your sputum tests have still been coming back positive. Moreover, after that episode yesterday afternoon in the gardens, well, you need one hundred percent bed rest for the next few weeks, maybe a month. And then I think it's safe to say you'll be completely rejuvenated, cured, and ready to head back on home, I assure you. Until then, any, and I mean *any*, arduous or stressful activities will be highly adverse and will worsen your condition tremendously and can be, if you'll forgive me for my dramatic vocabulary, quite life threatening. It's paramount that you take as much bed rest as possible and wait until the X-ray results come through. Okay, Sport?" he removed his spectacles, cleaned the lenses with a tissue, trying to stare me down.

I didn't say anything but reached into the pocket of my robe, took out a thick cash roll and placed it on the desk in front of him by the black telephone.

"Mr. Kel—Scott, as I said, I am dreadfully sorry, but I just can't let you leave here until you're deemed fully fit and fully cured. I won't have your health or God forbid your death or anyone else's for that matter, on my conscious. Not to mention the ethical code that I have to adhere to and here you are in my office forcing bribes on me. That's what it is, isn't it? Another one of your bribes?"

"I want your help getting a pass here, Doc. That's all. Think of the money as payment for services rendered."

His face grew very lined and he continued, "There has been talk on the ward of you wanting to leave here to look for an old flame. The woman from the newspapers? You know as well as I do what women are like, Sport; they are incredibly fickle creatures. She's more than likely down in Palm Springs in a spa. You know how these young women are sometimes. Not a thought for anyone else before they go gallivanting off into the sunset." He flashed that pearly-white, politician's smile at me, and cradling his fingers together.

I grabbed another roll from my robe pocket and tossed it onto the desk; it rolled against the desk lamp by his hand. His fingers started to tremble and twitch slightly, wanting to grab up that cool cash.

"Lord above, I could lose my medical license! I could lose my home. My wife would never forgive me… just so you can go and—forgive my vocabulary again—try to find some round-heels actress?! Who has probably been running around Los Angeles and Hollywood with anyone and everyone…"

The Doc looked like he was struggling to keep his composure, his bottom lip was trembling, but I was struggling to keep mine. My right eye ached. I could feel the anger building up at the back of my neck, perched on my shoulders, tightening, and tensing the muscles there. But I knew this was a situation where a good smack in the mouth or two wouldn't help me get what I wanted. I had to try another course of action.

"Doc, do you know Mickey Cohen?"

"Come again?"

"I asked, do you know Mickey Cohen?"

"The gangster?! Of course, I don't. I'm a medical professional not some kind of a—of a racketeer!"

"Well, Doc, I don't like to name-drop, but he is a good pal of mine."

"I will not be strong armed, Mr. Kelly! The first mobster type ruffian who shows up at the hospital, I'll call the police department straight away."

I went on, "Mickey Cohen likes to blackmail rich gentleman, like yourself, who stick their little pricks where they don't belong. Let's say, for example, in the cunnies of little post graduate nurses. I think your wife would be more than a little fucking disappointed to say the least, right, Doc? You won't be strong armed, but you will be extorted through the fucking ass. I'll make sure of that." I leaned forward, opened the sterling silver humidor on his desk, took out a cigar, and ran it along under my nose.

"Cuban? Nice, Doc." I bit off the tip, spat it on his colorful Persian rug and fumbled in my robe pocket for my Zippo lighter, then realized it was in my locker.

"You got a light, Doc?"

He squinted his blue eyes at me through the round, gold-framed lenses of his glasses like I had coughed up a hernia on his steak dinner. He patted down his hair, mumbled something under his breath and signed my release papers.

I'd never met Mickey Cohen before; I'd only spoken to him once over the telephone and he wasn't a pal. I had done one job and one job only for him in the past. A sort of win-win thing for the both of us. I'd had two associates who'd offered me jobs. Benjamin Siegel, who I didn't like all that much, because he acted like a vain, spoilt child. He always paid very well though, until the day I killed him. The other guy was Anthony Cornero, who people called 'The Admiral' because he used to own a small fleet of floating casinos before the government shut him down. I liked Anthony because he was a straight shooter and honest. An honest person in life is hard to find. Criminal life or civilian life, finding someone who tells it exactly how it is, is next to impossible.

I had mentioned Mickey Cohen to The Doc because guys like him needed to be made to feel insecure sometimes and what they didn't understand always made them feel insecure. I'd met his type in college, before the war. Sons of rich men thinking the rules weren't made for them. They called everyone "Sport". That's what life is to them, a sport, so I shined him on and told him what I needed to, the same way I did to everyone else.

"Thanks, Doc," I said, standing up. I used his marble desk-lighter to light up the cigar as he glared at me. I puffed on it a few times, coughed heavy and wet across the desk, snubbed the cigar out in an intricate glass ashtray and then went to get dressed into my civilian clothes.

I'd lost over sixty pounds since I'd been admitted into the sanatorium in April. My grey slacks, white shirt and blue sport coat didn't fit so great anymore, they hung in bunches from my body like rags on a scarecrow abandoned in a farmer's field.

"The last time I saw someone who looked like you do, I was freeing them from the Dachau concentration camp," Sinclair said.

I stared at myself in the long mirror attached to the door of my locker. My mousy hair greasy and swept back long on my skull. My cheekbones seemed to be stabbing their way through my ruddy features. The scars on the left side of my face pale and fleshy. My eyes a dull gunmetal, bloodshot and set deep in shadowed holes. The athletic and muscular body I had many months ago had gone to shit. I *did* look like one of those poor sons of bitches from Dachau.

"That's a grim, but true assessment, but you look pretty peaky yourself, Uncle Tom."

"I can't say, I'm sad to see you go, Cracker," he said, eyeing my brown, leather carrier case on the end of my bunk and then at the tiled flooring.

"You think you'll find her?" he asked.

"That or die trying," I said jokingly, but it sounded more like a pathetic prediction.

"The latter seems more than likely, in your condition, Lieutenant. But I wish you all the luck in the world," he said.

I coughed into my right hand, looked at the small flecks of blood and wiped it on my bed sheets. They'd seen worse and I'd not be using the bunk again.

"Thanks, I think maybe I'll need it."

"The newspapers said the last place she went to was her ex-husband's home, to talk about child support or alimony or some such thing. That might be a good place to start. The family always know something in these kinds of cases. You know the ex-husband at all?"

"Yeah, we've met a couple of times."

"Will he be helpful to you?"

"No. That's not likely. But I'm sure he'll come around with some encouragement."

"You know Lieutenant, I'm sorry to say it to you, but maybe some women are better gone. Better not found. You see what I'm saying to you? Maybe, you're better off letting the cops deal with the situation. Maybe, you know, it's a dangerous world, is all I'm saying. We both know that. What I'm trying to say, Lieutenant, is have you really thought about if she has run off with another fella or even worse, God forbid it, if she's dead?"

"Not this woman, Sinclair. Not her. I know she isn't dead. She's just got into something or something bad has happened.

She's out there somewhere and she needs me. I know it. She's waiting for me. I need… I need to know. I can't think about any other possibilities at this moment."

"Well, you won't be doing your health any favors. I hope this girl is worth it."

"She is," I said.

Sinclair tried to smile, faltered at it, then lay back down on his bunk sighing heavily, the way only a tired man can. I shook his hand firmly, picked up my brown case, and walked slowly out of the B Ward not speaking to anyone else. I had no one else to say goodbye to. I looked over at Sinclair once again as I went through the door towards the reception area. He was still laid propped up on a pillow, reading a newspaper and slowly shaking his head. I had a feeling I would never see him again.

ALL THE PATIENTS from the A Ward were outside in their white, blanketed bunks. It was always surreal to see them like that. Patients in cribs that were outside, underneath the sky. The nurses and doctors moved them out there underneath the sun-bleached Spanish arches of the main entrance on sunny, dry days. They believed the fresh air would aid in their recovery. I felt their many eyes on me, squinting in the late morning light, as I walked slowly to the main gate. No one smiled when I looked back at the passive faces. I didn't blame them. They were death row inmates watching an escapee walking to freedom. Fuck them.

I shuffled through the red bricked posts of the main gate and walked slowly down the street for twenty minutes. I had to stop, sit down, and rest a number of times. Out of breath and exhausted already. It was the furthest I'd walked in six months. No taxicabs in sight. There never were when you really needed one. Panting like a mutt and drenched in a cold sweat, I sat down at a bus stop with a bench and waited for one to take me home. The breeze cool on my skin, I thought about Jean and what I would say to her when I found her. Although I had more questions than statements.

Riding the bus back into the old neighborhood seemed like a reprieve. A smooth and relaxing ride. I took off my sport coat, folded it, and placed it on top of my case on the seat beside me. The sweat on the back of my shirt and armpits dried out as I looked out the window, watching for Jean. I thought I saw her coming out of a store, holding brown papers bags under each arm. In an automat drinking a coffee by the window. Walking a small black dog on a short purple leash. It was never her. Spinning with vertigo and disorientated, I calmed myself down by concentrating on leveling my breathing and heart beat out. Counting backwards in my head like the nurses had taught me to do when I was on the verge of a coughing fit. A psychological aid, they'd said. Sometimes it worked, other times it didn't. You couldn't prevent a coughing fit, only try to delay it until later, like most of life's bullshit.

A few stops later, a bunch of preppy schoolboys in blue-plaid uniforms got on the bus and chattered away like monkeys. One of them saw me, whispered to another, who passed it on, and a heavy hush settled over them. Children are much more observant than adults. They're the first to spot someone out of place. In this case a skeleton man, coughing incessantly, wearing ill-fitting, blood-peppered clothes. I scowled at them and winked. They got off the bus at the very next stop. Beth, my ex-wife, had told me once that any man who rode the bus after the age of thirty was a loser in life. I wish she could have seen me then. She always loved to be right.

My daughter's ninth birthday had been the month before. I'd written a long letter to her from the sanatorium and enclosed it with some cash in a card. I didn't know if she'd received it or not, but I hoped she did and smiled at the doodles I'd drawn at the edges of the letter. I hope she bought herself something nice with the money. When I received no reply, I wrote another letter to Beth to ask how she was and how our daughter was getting along in New York and her new school. I didn't receive a reply to that letter either. It's funny how quickly you can go from being the somebody to a nobody in a woman's eyes and in her heart. I knew my daughter was better without me, but I hoped I was still somebody to her. I closed my eyes and saw her there, but she was crying. Her mother braiding her hair at a breakfast bar and she was shouting "Daddy!" The smell of gunpowder and blood. My breathing started up erratic. My heart convulsed. I thought about Jean to ease my breathing back out. Jean and I in a Palm Springs hotel. I imagined finding her. Kissing her again. Feeling her skin underneath my fingertips again. I was somebody for Jean. She loved me. I had nothing good in my life without Jean, just a shitty bar, a lot of bad memories, and the fucking consumption.

While the bus jostled down the avenues and streets, stalling in traffic occasionally, I tried to formulate a strategy to search for Jean. A battle plan to find her. I couldn't talk to the cops in the shape I was in. They would take one look at me and ship me back to the sanatorium. What sway I'd held with the LAPD was all but ruined on my last job for Benny Siegel. Nonexistent when they finally tied the toe tag on him. Sinclair had reminded me that the newspaper had reported that Jean went to see her ex-husband, Dexter, before she disappeared. That had to be as good a place to start as any. Dexter wouldn't shop me to the cops, even if I had to get a little rough with him. I'd cowed him before; I could do it again. Even with the tuberculosis. Dexter was the kind of guy who constantly wrote checks with his fat mouth that his weak spine couldn't cash. He always had his big beak in Jean's business after the divorce. Had private detectives tailing her around and snooping in our relationship until I had to put one of the dicks in the hospital, quickly followed after by Dexter with a broken arm. Jean was given custody of her daughter shortly after that and I became a hero in her eyes for a while. Dexter was a coward, but he knew how to play ball and I knew he'd know more than he was telling the cops or the tabloid newspapers about Jean's disappearance. He had to. Dexter, my only link to Jean. I thought about how pathetic that seemed and then I realized I hadn't actually met any of Jean's friends or family. I couldn't name a single friend or acquaintance of hers. I didn't know anyone she knew. I didn't know anything about her family except she hated her father and hated her mother more. She lived with her mother, brother, and sister-in-law and said it was hell. She told them nothing about her private life. They'd call the cops as soon as they saw me walking up the garden path because they thought I'd abused Jean, so it'd be no good trying those fucking yokels. I didn't know much of Jean's upbringing either. She'd told me she'd grown up in Seattle and had come to Los Angeles when she was in high school, which she'd not attended all that much after she'd been raped by members of the football team. Said she'd had a lot of no good relationships with a lot of no good men and a shitty marriage to a shitty husband, but that's all I knew about her. And that was about her past. What I knew about her present I could have scribbled on the inside of a matchbook cover. How could it be possible to know a woman so intimately yet hardly really know her at all? Was it my fault? Did she tell me things and I'd not been listening?

I attempted to recollect something, remember anything, but every time I closed my eyes to try, I saw the way she smiled. She smiled using her whole face. Those eyes. I remembered how she stood making coffee in the morning wearing only her panties. Her breasts naked and firm, pinkish nipples hardened in the cool morning air. I saw the way she frowned and pouted her lips when she would reach climax tightening her legs so powerfully, holding me pleasantly captive there. Or the way her long chestnut hair would twist and roll across the white linen bedsheets as the sunrise lit up my room. The way she'd take a cigarette from my mouth, smoke a little, exhale the smoke through a girlish grin and pass it back to me. I could see all those things, but they were the only personal things I knew of her. I wondered what kind of a relationship it was. I wondered who needed who more? Who had been using who more? I had always thought we were both using each other to some degree. Like all romantic relationships have the habit of becoming after you've become comfortable with each other's company.

I'd always been a sucker for a beautiful face, but I'd gone deep into a black hole with this woman and lost myself there.

Sinclair might've been right after all, maybe Jean hadn't visited me in the hospital the last few months because she was finally done with me this time. I'd pushed her away with my behavior in The Doc's office her last visit. Maybe I was on a bus to nowhere. She loved me though. I was certain of that. I'd felt it. What it all came down to was needing to know. I had to be sure she was safe. Most of all, I needed to know I wasn't lying to myself. Shining myself on. Grabbing my Zippo lighter from the pocket of my slacks, I read the inscription on it over and over like a Hail Mary. Then I gazed out of the window, taking a break from thinking and watched Los Angeles bustling by. Stopping when Jean's face appeared to be everywhere and in everything. I thought about the first time she'd been gone.

CHRISTMAS DAY, '47. We had been opening presents all morning. Drinking and fucking all afternoon. A lazy Christmas Day spent in bed, making love. Jean had been wearing a new necklace the whole time. Pearls. Expensive. Not a gift from me. Nor from her ex-husband. He had hated her after he found out about us, blamed me for their divorce. Jean and him only kept the divorce amicable, with my guidance, for their young daughter. I'd given her a diamond necklace a few months back for her twenty-fourth birthday and she'd worn it every day since. I was thrown and pissed to see a replacement around her throat. I had spotted the pearls straight away the night before. Had watched them bounce and ripple on her neck as I was on top of her. Reflecting the light and burning holes through my head. I'd endured the pearls because I didn't want to fight. When the next morning, I couldn't bear it any longer, I casually asked her who'd given her the new, expensive necklace around her neck. She'd touched the pearls quickly, startled, as though she'd forgotten she was wearing them. Told me they were a gift from her mother when she first left home for California. Another one of her bald-faced lies. She lied and continued to lie. We both became hysterical. The old rage came flooding back and the more she lied to my face, the angrier I became. I lost control of myself. That one time. I lost my mind with her and I smacked her, once. Mostly out of frustration. She smacked me around a little too. The Christmas tree was smashed. Vases and glasses too. A wine bottle thrown by Jean, broke my cheekbone.

Neighbors called the cops. Two officers showed up knocking at the front door. They realized who I was and who I worked for. They became polite, they apologized and then they left the scene with an extra Christmas bonus each. That's what happened. Of course, I'd regretted the fight later. I always regretted the fights after they'd happened. There's only so much a woman will take before she goes to another man. The whole fight had been a convenient excuse for her to leave me, I thought bitterly after, sat in my wrecked house alone. The same trick Jean had pulled with her ex-husband when she left him for me. She'd broken our relationship off with a slammed door and I had swept it up with the other broken glass and crockery. She moved on quickly to someone new, the way all beautiful women seem to do.

In the weeks after, driven crazy from being without Jean, I became weak. I pleaded with her. Begged her. She ignored my phone calls and letters. I went to the clubs she danced in and was told she'd quit. People said she'd started courting other guys. A lot of them. Words like a bullet in the fucking guts. When she did finally contact me via a letter I'd found crumpled in my mailbox, she wrote I was cramping her style. Embarrassing myself. I was pathetic. I knew the relationship had become toxic, but like all good medicines, I needed her. I was a junkie for her. She was my morphine. I turned L.A upside down searching for her. I didn't hear anything. Nothing. Then a few months later and a year before I got the consumption, she must have had her heart broken or lost interest in the others because she returned to me. I didn't care why she was back. She always came back, and I always took her back. Jean who came in and out of my life like a stray cat escaping the cold. Always hungry and always needing me the very same way I needed her. We always started over at the beginning. Full circle. A cycle of the dead fucking the dead. Ghosts haunting ghosts.

A COUPLE OF old ladies well into the later stages of their sixties squawking opposite to me about Jean's disappearance pulled me out of my head.

"Oh, it's simply terrible, isn't it?"

"Oh yes, simply awful. And such a pretty young thing too."

"I do hope they find her safe and well. Poor thing. There's a lunatic attacking young girls, you know? He cut that other woman in half and left her naked as the day she was born by the side of the street in one of those ugly abandoned lots. It's an awful business."

"Oh yes, I heard about that, a couple of years ago, 1947, wasn't it? Oh yes, I heard about that one for sure. A werewolf, they'd said on the news. Awful, awful business. They never found the man that did it. It's dreadful."

"Yes, an utterly dreadful business, of course."

"They say a salesgirl at the Farmers Market saw the poor little thing loitering in the store for hours almost as though she was waiting for someone to pick her up."

"No doubt she was up to no good then. Loitering around like that."

"What do you mean, Elsa?"

"Well, I heard she worked in that dreadful sin pit Hollywood. What more is there to say about those types of girls? Hollywood starlets? More like Hollywood harlots, the lot of them."

"Oh, dear Lord. You don't say?"

"Oh, yes. Those pretty, young women have to literally sell their bodies to get parts in those pictures. At least, that's what I have heard."

"Oh, and I heard she often went to clubs that played the negro music."

"Oh, dear Lord. That's just asking for trouble to come knocking at your door, isn't it?"

"I read in the tabloid newspapers that she was here one minute and gone the next, the same as that Judge Crater fellow."

"Really? That's eerie. Wherever could she have gone too?"

"Run away from her responsibilities with a man, I suspect. Across the border and into Mexico." They realized I was listening, ended their conversation abruptly and eyed me suspiciously. Perhaps, thinking I was the werewolf that they'd read about. My final stop was coming up, so I decided to have a little fun with the old hags. I breathed really deep and coaxed a wet cough up. The taste of iron filled my mouth. Let some of the blood dribble down from my lips, onto my chin and into my stubble, eyes bulging across at them.

"Good evening ladies. You're both looking swell. Just swell indeed," I growled.

They let out gassy, horrified gasps and tried to push themselves deeper into their seats. I stood up and leaned over them menacingly. One of them began to whimper.

My ex-wife always did love to be right.

I swayed and stumbled off the bus, falling to my knees on the sidewalk of Fairfax Avenue.

I was finally back home. My piece of Ireland. My bar.

CHAPTER 4

THE BAR WAS actually on the corner of Fairfax Avenue and Santa Monica Boulevard. A faded brick building with a large semi-circle window under the stone eaves of the flat roof which looked out and over the palm tree lined avenue from the small one-room apartment upstairs. The Jew deli that adjoined it was built in exactly the same architectural style, as was the Chinese dry cleaners on the other side and many of the other places down the avenue. I'd always thought the three storefronts would have made a grand joke. A Jew deli, an Irish bar, and a Chink dry cleaners. I'd never been able to think of a good enough punchline though.

The neon shamrock sign above the door still wasn't working and the bar windows looked as though they hadn't been cleaned since I'd left. Some witty drunk had written in the grime on the glass of one window, *'I wish my wife was this dirty!'*. Cleaning the windows of the bar would have been the job of the kid I'd left in charge. His name was Charlie and he'd served under me in my platoon when we had been Marines. Barely out of school and too young and stupid to know better. He'd been the baby of the platoon and even the youngest in the battalion. A lot of the guys had looked out for him because they felt bad for the guy. They thought he was a retard, so they were big brother protective of him. I sometimes wondered if he was a retard too, but he seemed a good enough kid and I was protective of him as well. He had a heart that was too clean and pure for a war, especially a war as dirty and cruel as Okinawa had been.

One day after we had taken Shuri Castle in the heart of Okinawa, the war all but finished, he'd gotten drunk on moonshine and the guys had started razzing him as usual. He started bitching about how he'd got no kills, so I and a few of the others took him over to where we held the prisoners in a bamboo cage wrapped in barbed wire to pop his cherry. A bunch of trembling, sick, skin and bone, pathetic Japs stared out at us. Gazing through the bars like stray dogs in the pound. We'd dragged them out of the makeshift prison one by one, pushed and pulled them over to the large pit we'd dug in the muddy earth and lined them up. The Japs didn't cry or moan. They stared, as resigned to the consequences by then, as I was resigned to the actions. I'd held out my Colt 1911 pistol to Charlie, said this was his chance to get a live kill and the poor kid had started blubbering like a baby. He didn't have the gumption. I'd been the same when I'd first arrived. I had to admit that I envied him and despised him for still being that way. I shot each Jap once in the face. We made Charlie fill in the pit after as a kind of punishment and we watched him sobbing miserably as he'd done it, a few of the guys still razzing him. It was something I'd regretted a lot after.

After the war he had returned to his hometown in Detroit. Become a barfly, started riding the rails around America and later tracked me down in California looking for help. Some trouble he'd got into because of a young girl, he'd said. No, Charlie wasn't the sharpest tool in the box, but the kid was loyal to a fault and good. He had no family and no friends, so I had taken him in feeling responsible for him still.

I'd given him a job and the back room of the bar to put a cot in, furnished him with an old locker to use as his own. Taught him everything I knew about running a bar, which took all of five or ten minutes. In the beginning he'd kept hassling me about letting him come along with me on a job from the Italians or the Jews. Make introductions for him. He had read too many pulps and wanted to be the next Al Capone. I told him to work the bar and pour the drinks. When I'd become sick, I'd put him in charge of the place while I was gone. It looked as though he'd not done much of anything since I'd been in the sanatorium.

I pushed open the door and was greeted with that bar stink

that was there wherever you went in the world. An international odor. Piss, stale beer, and old tobacco. The place empty except for Charlie sat behind the bar, reading a pulp magazine with his feet up on the cash register picking at his small upturned nose with his pinky finger. I didn't want to shout or talk too much, because I was exhausted and felt a fever coming on. I walked right up to him, put my hand on his arm and gripped it faintly. He let out a muffled girlish scream and fell off his barstool.

"Someone's gonna get eighty-sixed with honors, you — Lieutenant Scott?! I'm sorry! I didn't know it was you— You're back?!"

"I'm back, but I'm just visiting for a little while."

"You're not kicking me out, are you?"

"No, of course not, Kid."

"That's good, cos' I've got no other place to go. I need this place. And anyway, I've been looking after the place well, like I promised."

I looked at the filth on the bar and on the floors.

"Yeah, Charlie. It sure looks like it."

"I mean… It's great to see you, Lieutenant. I'm sorry. You wanna drink or something?"

"Yeah, I might as well."

"The usual, right?"

"Yeah, but no ice."

"That's good, cos' we're all out of ice. I've been meaning to get more," he poured whisky into a cracked glass and I gulped it down my throat.

"Another."

He filled up another and I poured that one down my throat too.

"Fuck you, consumption," I said.

"I'll drink to fuck consumption, too," Charlie said, pouring himself four fingers.

"To dead buddies."

We tapped our glasses together.

"To the dead."

I could feel my chest heating up, then boiling. An arsonist sprinting around inside of me, setting house fires in my lungs.

"Those whiskies are going to cost me, I think."

"Don't be silly, Lieutenant Scott. This is your place. The drinks are on the house, of course, right?"

I looked at him and almost laughed, but instead started heaving and then hacking. I got an old bar rag to my mouth and coughed it up. It was getting worse than it had ever been before. The Doc had been right. It had been a long day and I'd done too much. My right eye ached. I saw black spots, flies on the insides of my vision and only had time to tell Charlie to help me up the stairs to my apartment before I passed out.

SUNLIGHT SHONE THROUGH the skin of my eyelids the brightest yellow. I could smell a sweet aroma all around me. I yawned and stretched. Opened my eyes. Squinted. The bed was a mess of tangled sheets. I lay there sleepily, watching Jean across the room in the small kitchen alcove. Naked except for my white undershirt, her long wavy hair falling in coffee-colored ripples down her back, frying something in a pan.

"Good morning. What're you cooking up?" I grinned, rubbed at my crusty eyes.

"Good morning, Scotty, Sweetheart. I'm making pancakes."

"Pancakes?"

"Uh-huh, I know you're not too fond of eggs and I think there's no better way to wake up and start the day than pancakes and fresh coffee, right?"

"Well, I'm sure we could both think of some things much better than pancakes and coffee."

She placed a hand on a pushed-out hip and a finger to her pouting lips in mock consideration. Her pussy hair wild and golden brown in the morning light.

"Mmm, I can't. Sorry, Sweetheart," the tip of her tongue flashed through her lips.

"Oh, yeah?" I kicked the bed sheets to the floor.

"Yeah, that's right, Mister."

"Maybe, I should give you something to contemplate."

"The pancakes will burn."

"I'll be quick."

"That's not a romantic proposition in the slightest, Scotty."

She went back to poking at the pan with a fork. Pouting.

I got out of the bed and walked the seven paces it took to the kitchen. Wrapped my arms around her from behind, massaging her breasts, feeling her nipples firm. Kissed her neck under the ear, the way she liked. Tasting the odor of last night's perfume and the perspiration on her skin.

"Scotty, I said the pancakes will burn, cut it out," she playfully elbowed me. I ran my fingertips down past her navel, through the thickness of hair. Slid my fingers down and then back up the moist canal, to that special spot. Jean let out a gasp, a sigh, her thighs trembled. I spun her around roughly and pushed, walked her up against the sink. She raised her leg up and over my hip. I slid myself inside her, feeling her body relent and then yield to me further, my mouth on hers. Together. Full circle.

The pancakes were black rocks by the time we had finished, and grey smoke filled the apartment. We lay in bed again, collapsed into a tangled mess of contentment and satisfaction. The breeze streamed through the open windows over our naked damp bodies. Jean twisted the diamond necklace I'd given her between her fingertips.

"When are you going to stay over at my place? I want you to meet my daughter and I know she'd love you. I just know it. We always stay here, Scotty. I mean, it's nice but I'm starting to think you don't want to come to mine."

"I will. Sure. I want to see your place and meet your kid, of course," I lied.

"Well, okay then… Did you sleep well, last night?" she said, tracing her fingertips on my chest, making shapes of things.

"Yeah, I did. Like a babe."

"That's good. I've been a little worried about you recently, Scotty."

"Me? Why?" I chuckled but my guts dropped.

"You don't sleep so well, sometimes. But recently it's gotten worse. Don't you think? You should talk to someone about the bad dreams. Or those scary daydreams you have sometimes."

"What? No, I don't need to talk to anyone. You want me to talk to some fucking quack about my feelings?" I forced another chuckle. "It's fine. Put the radio on, Jean. Let's listen to something."

"I'm worried about you, Scotty. I want to help you. I want you to be happy."

"I am happy, Jean."

"How about the veteran's hospital? You could talk to someone there."

"I said I'm okay, Jean. So, let's change the fucking subject alright?"

"Don't be like that, Scotty. I just wanna help you."

"You're helping me, Jean."

"How?"

"Like just now in the kitchen," I grinned, kissed her forehead.

"So, that's all I'm good for? A quick fuck on the kitchen sink? Thanks, Scott. I feel really special now," she went to roll over, turn her back to me, pouting. I pulled her close. Kissed her neck.

"You are special. Really."

"More than your ex-wife and daughter?"

"I said you're special, Jean."

"I want to feel like I'm more to you. More than this," she waved her hands at her naked body.

"You are. You are, Jean. So much more."

"I want you to love me, Scotty."

I got on top of her, kissed her mouth and she turned her head away. I spat on my fingers, moistened, and pushed myself into her. She didn't refuse, but she didn't reciprocate. I didn't stop. She relaxed and let me in. I slid into her as she avoided eye contact, squeezing her eyes shut making lines on her face as though she'd aged suddenly. I kissed her pouting lips and she kissed back, said "okay". She was Okinawa and I was the

American forces. I wanted to break her down and conquer her. I wanted to occupy her lands. I wanted to occupy Jean fully and finally. I saw tears glisten at the corners of her closed eyes, I kissed them there, but didn't stop. I wanted to make her only mine. She wanted me to tell her something. I wanted to tell her. I didn't know why I couldn't.

I WOKE UP with closed eyes, almost peacefully from a dreamless sleep. The best kind of sleep. The rarest kind of rest. The sounds of the morning traffic like an ocean tide outside on the street below. Jean had been gone seven days now. Seven days. I wondered what she was doing at that moment. Was she back in Wilshire? Maybe, she'd come back. I made a mental note to check the newspapers and the radio. I heard a creaking sound, opened my eyes, startled and saw Charlie sat at the bottom of the bed on a rickety chair by the door, spinning my 1911 Colt pistol on his finger like a retarded Lone Ranger. The sun shining on his screwed-up face, he looked shell-shocked. Wide eyed and blank. He wasn't in the room; somewhere else. I knew where. For the first time after the war, I really looked at Charlie. He seemed haggard and tormented. His skin was oily with an unhealthy yellowish tinge. His muddy hair stuck out like a duck's ass on his greasy forehead and he had an outbreak of herpes on his lower lip. He was obviously struggling. I wanted to ask him how he was coping emotionally, how he felt about the past, but we were men and men didn't ask such things of other men.

"Charlie what the hell are you doing? Put that back where you got it. Put it back in the cigar box."

"You're awake Lieutenant Scott. I was doing sentry duty. You know? Like before, in Okinawa. I was acting like your bodyguard, protecting you while you were sleeping."

"That's good, Kid. Now put the pistol back in the cigar box where you got it from."

He stared at me for a long moment. His eyes red and bloodshot. No, I thought, he didn't look like he was coping well at all. He kept licking his thick blueish lips and I knew he was working his way up to ask something that he thought was of the deepest importance and deeply existential, but often turned out to be the complete opposite. I had known that long stare and lip licking from the war.

"Do you think I'm a sissy, Lieutenant Scott? Some sort of a nance?"

There it was, that small fear that crept slouching at the back of insecure men's minds, the awful fear of being thought of as a weak sister or a sissy. Was there any slur worse for a man? A lot of violence and heinous acts had probably been done to avoid such insecurities. Some men had gone to wars to avoid such, killed others in wars to avoid such and finally, in the end, went to their own deaths to avoid such.

"Huh? Kid, of course not. Why would you even ask me something ridiculous like that?"

"I could've killed those dirty Nips that day. Put a bullet right through their fucking little eyes. You know that, right?" he lifted the pistol up, pretended to shoot the bookcase across the room and then blew on the barrel comic book style.

He continued, "Yeah, I could've killed them, but I didn't want to, cos' they were prisoners of war. You shouldn't kill prisoners of war, even if they are only Nips; it's against a convention or something. That's why I didn't do it. I could've though. I could've. I really could've."

"Okay, Charlie, it doesn't matter now anyway, and you did good, Kid. You're not a bad person."

"You think I'm weak, Lieutenant. I know it. You think I don't have what it takes. You think I'm too soft."

"No, I think you're a good guy, Charlie. That's what I think. You're a good guy."

"I could be like you, Lieutenant. I could kill bad guys."

"Good guys don't kill bad guys, Charlie. Bad guys kill other bad guys and then they get fucking killed themselves. It's a never-ending circle of bullshit and blood. Worse than the war. Now put the God-damned pistol back in the fucking cigar box and fetch me a glass of water, will you?"

He walked over to the shelf, put the Colt back in the cigar box and shut the lid, licking his lips again.

"How come you still have it anyway? The pistol? You were supposed to give it back and sign your name when they sent us home. I did that with my rifle. It's the rules, Lieutenant."

"I told them that I lost it at Sugar Loaf Hill."

"And they fell for that baloney?"

"I still have it, don't I?"

"You broke the rules?"

"Yeah, I guess I might've. But fuck it. Fuck them all, Charlie."

I sat up, took out a stale cigarette from a six-month-old pack of Luckies on the bedside table, lit it with my Zippo and tried to smoke it. I inhaled once, coughed painfully a few times, and snuffed it out in the ashtray. I wiped my mouth with the bedsheet.

"I don't think you should be smoking cigarettes, Lieutenant Scott."

"I know. I know," I threw the packet to Charlie. He tried to catch it but fumbled and dropped it. I lay back down and read the inscription on the lighter.

'From the one, who loves you most.'

I squeezed the lighter in my palm until it hurt. Holding it to my chest.

"You know? I know why you're back," Charlie slumped back down in the chair.

"Because I needed one of your cocktails? One of your Bloody Marys?"

"No, I think you came back to look for that woman. I read about her in the newspapers. Jean Spangler. She was the woman who was always around here with you months and months back. I remembered her cos' of that one time you introduced me to her, but I was too shy, so I went to my room. I always went to my room when she was here. Well, I know that she's disappeared, and the newspapers think the Black Dahlia Killer got to her. I can help you, Lieutenant Scott. I can scout, run point, and help you and if anyone tries any kind of funny business, well, I'll put them in the ground. I'll kill them dead if you give me another chance. I'll show you that I've got what it takes. I'll show you I've got the gumption, Lieutenant Scott."

My throat was dry, I was thirsty, I needed to take a piss and I was exhausted by Charlie already. I'd forgotten how draining he could be at times.

"I need you to go and get me a glass of water, Charlie. That's all I need from you. You'll stay here and look after the bar. And for God's sake, mop the floors, clean the windows, and empty the ashtrays every once in a while, will you?"

He pulled a sullen face at a crack in the ceiling like a child and stamped out of the room. I laid my head on the pillow and listened to him slowly bang down the stairs. I lifted the blankets to my nose and imagined I could still smell Jean's perfume there, could taste it there. We'd made love in this bed so often, in this room so often, that the bed and the room belonged to her. It all belonged to her. The walls, the bed, the bookshelves, the books, the chair, the small kitchen, the sink. Everything. She had left a lingering energy here in the room. I wondered where she was and what she was doing? She had been gone seven days. Seven days.

A little while later, I could sit up without feeling too shaky. Stand up without feeling too shaky. Walk around the room without feeling too shaky. So, I stumbled to the WC, took a piss, went to the bathroom, showered, brushed my teeth, and put on some fresh clothes. By the time I finished my heart was pounding, drenched in a cold sweat and my breath was wheezing. Lightheaded. Seasick. I fell down in the chair. Looked out of the window. I couldn't breathe and my vision was growing ocean colored cloudy. Jean had been missing seven days. Seven days. I could smell someone frying eggs somewhere. Breaking eggs on the lip of a pan and frying them...

That child's nursery rhyme again.

Okinawa again.

The movie reel clicks on and lights up the empty stage.

HILL 60 AGAIN. The Sugar Loaf Hill they had called it. A demented name for what it was. A little over two weeks and some since we had landed on that island, since we had landed in that hellish machine that ground us into bloody minced meat. A lot of men were wounded. Some men were dead. My Division and Japs. My Battalion mostly. I had somehow survived. I hadn't been killed. I hadn't killed. A compromise I'd made with myself.

I was dug into the ground again. A foxhole. Scared to move a muscle. My uniform was rotted on my body and infested with lice and fleas. Rashes over my skin. The smell of shit and blood floated through the air on black skinned wings, danced the Lindy Hop with the screams of so many young men. Brave men finally reduced in the end to crushed, broken things that cried out for "Mommy" and "Medic" in the burning morning sun. Mommy was dead and the Medic had blown his brains out the night before.

The Japs had fortified themselves into the hill, buried deep in caves like ticks, dug in, they cut us down with machine gun fire like dead grass and crawled out of the dirt at night to kill the ones of us who were lucky enough to die while they dreamed. They sent civilians out of their holes and caves at the ends of rifles to fetch water and food. The civilians, women, and children mostly, were cut to pieces by our infuriated, petrified, and nervous gunfire, before they'd even seen the sunlight fully. I watched them die. They died badly. I didn't want to die like that. I didn't want to die at all. I won't kill you. Don't kill me. A compromise.

We were all bleeding. The grass was bleeding. The dust on the ground was bleeding. Okinawa was bleeding. My face was sticky with sweat and tears and I hid it in the dirt and grass, so none of the other men would see me weeping. I had never prayed before, but I was praying then. I Prayed to God. I prayed to the Devil. I prayed; I would side with whoever could get me out of that shit. I would give my soul to whoever could get me out of that shit. A mangy looking crow flew down and picked at a dead Marine's eye as the corpse smirked at the sky. The crow twisted its neck towards me and looked. Its eyes like drops of oil smirked too. It winked at me and flew blackly away.

The orders came down from the top. I knew they would. With a fistful of men and a fistful of bullets we were to take that hill. That small, insignificant hill crawling with Japs. The Sugar Loaf. No… no reinforcements, there were none. There was no one left. I had passed the orders onto the leftovers of my platoon with a breaking, almost apologetic tone of voice. Hill 60. Sugar Loaf Hill. Before the sun had fallen take that hill. By hook or crook take that fucking hill. For the red, white and blue. For your friends, for your buddies. For all patriotic, vapid bullshit. Before dusk we fixed bayonets and we attacked. It was our own kamikaze banzai charge.

HERE HE WAS. My oldest friend. Again. My first friend. No better friend, no worse enemy. Machine gun fire all around us, buzzing like a plague of mosquitoes. He had been waiting for me there again in the ruptured earth of the hill. He had always been waiting there. Mortars punched the shaking earth, ripped it into shards. A swamp of smoke like blindness. The Japs counterattacked. They ran at us like we were all friends. And there, in that place we were all the oldest of friends. He and I collided in the confusion. Pulling and grabbing, rolling together, rapists in the lunatic asylum. Don't kill me. I won't kill you. My oldest friend. I lost my grip on my Thompson and it tumbled away from me into a patch of yellow grass. We sat on our asses facing each other then. We could have been anywhere in the world. The oldest of friends. Shooting the shit. *How's your family? Father was hit by a streetcar while he was drunk. He is dying in the charity ward. My daughter is sick with pneumonia, we don't have enough money for the medical bills. My woman is gone. Have you seen her around anywhere?* Don't kill me. I won't kill you, oldest friend. He should have been a schoolboy, not a soldier. Shaved, brown, little round head. Shocked and stupefied in a dirty, baggy, khaki uniform. Too young to have known any woman's caress but his mother's. His teeth were very white and stuck out goofily from his lips. In elementary school the children in his class had teased him about it. He loved a girl who married another. He was very mournful. *Don't kill me. I won't kill you.* He brandished his rifle to his chest like a security blanket. He contemplated my weapon, harmless and out of reach in the yellowed grass over there, a million miles away. He gaped into my eyes, looking dejected and very mournful. Everywhere and everything was a screaming mess. And, then he screamed too, rose to stick me with his bayoneted rifle. He had a very mournful face. I swung off my helmet. Smashed it into his features. He screamed again, but it was a different kind of scream. I was on him then. He screamed again, that different kind. I screamed too. I brought my helmet down again and again and again. He had a very mournful face and I brought my helmet down on it again and again. His face broke apart like an egg in my hands. He was my oldest friend. Something inside me had stopped.

I REMEMBERED EATING watermelon with my mother in our front yard. The watermelon was very sticky and wet in my hands. I always felt very safe in my mother's arms. I was ten years old and she held me. In her arms she held me, nothing could hurt me there. She was wearing a long cotton dress. It was blue. Blood soaked into the fabric and spread. I could hear the ocean.

Birds sang so slowly.

A little girl screamed for her Daddy.

It was always so red, white, and blue. I was so angry that he had a very mournful face. *Why were you so sad little boy? You're going home and school is finished for the summer. Yes, I know, things fall apart; the center cannot hold*; the smell of smoke, shit and blood was in the air...

I SNAPPED OPEN my eyes, retching into the toilet bowl. A taste in my mouth of copper coins. My hair hanging in the brackish, pinkish water. Face wet, my eyes stung. My breathing sounded claustrophobic in my throat, as though I were breathing through a pin hole. I brought my fist down on the floorboards again and again and again until Charlie came up the stairs and found me. He placed a plate of fried eggs hurriedly on the bed. I vomited.

"Can't handle your liquor, huh, Lieutenant?" he giggled.

He helped me to my feet. An elation radiated from him like heat from a stove. He felt as though he had won something important. What it was I didn't know. He tried to walk me to the bed, but I pointed to the chair. Another fit of coughs rolled out, I sat down heavily and motioned to a grey rag on the floor. He snatched it up and tossed it to me. There was a glass of water next to the bed that Charlie had put there at some time, I didn't know when. I quickly took it, pouring it over the rag and held it over my mouth and nose. Counting slowly in my head. Feeling my body start to unclamp and release.

"Are you okay, Lieutenant?"

"I… I'm… okay," I wheezed it out. Hoarse.

"That sure is a lot of blood. I don't think I've ever seen that much blood here at home. Except, maybe, when I had a nosebleed once or when that girl… Are you dying, Lieutenant Scott?"

"No. I don't know. I don't think so. Not yet. Do you remember 'Waltzing Matilda'?"

"Huh, why of course. How could I forget our battle song? Still remember when we all first heard it on R and R in Australia. We heard it and then our whole battalion use to sing it all the time. Day and night. We had a good time there, in Australia, huh?"

He began to sing; "Waltzing Matilda. Waltzing Matilda."

"Stop. Just fucking stop singing."

"What's wrong, Lieutenant Scott? I think, maybe, it would be best if I called the hospital, got them to come and collect you again, you're not well at all. Not well at all. No, sir."

I shook my head and grabbed his arm hard as he went to walk away towards the door.

"No. Fucking. Hospitals. Charlie."

He pulled his arm away and rubbed at it. A hurt look on his face.

"Well, jeez, there's no call for that, Lieutenant Scott. It's just that you can't help that woman, you can't even help yourself. Look at you, especially when you want to do everything on your lonesome and without my help." He stood there with his hands on his hips. Probably in an imitation of something he'd seen a teacher do when he was a kid in high school. His idea of what an authority figure should have looked like. I'd never realized how lanky he looked. Gangly and all sharp edges.

"Charlie, just get me a telephone directory. For Los Angeles."

"Not until you say you need my help. You need me to help you save that woman and maybe I'll have to fight. Maybe I'll have to kill. I can do it. You need me, Lieutenant Scott."

"Charlie, do you have anywhere to go, if I eighty-six you from this bar?"

Suddenly his whole demeanor changed. He put his hands up to his face. Rounded his shoulders. Cowed.

"No, Lieutenant Scott. You know, I don't got nowhere. This is my home now. I can't go back to Detroit cos' of that trouble with that stupid liar, slutty girl… I told you about it."

"If you don't look after the bar, you're eighty-sixed. You understand? The bar is your job. It's your job, now. Your responsibility. You finally get it, Kid? I don't want your help. You haven't got the gumption and you know it. That's why we made you fill in that pit with the dead Japs, because that's all you were good for. You were no use for anything. Now go and get me a… Telephone. Directory. Now!" The last three words came out with hacking coughs again.

He stood there wavering, glaring at me, a sneer on his face. At that moment he reminded me a lot of something he did in the war. I felt a cold, solid weight hit me in the bottom of my stomach and spread there like internal bleeding. I couldn't remember what it had been. Something about a dice game. A group of soldiers from our platoon shooting dice in a huddled group, they were cheering, and I'd seen something in Charlie that I had hated. I couldn't remember what it had been though. It was lost with all the other terrible shit I'd seen in the war and since then.

"Please, Charlie," I said softer.

His childlike anger and sneer dissipated as quickly as they had arisen. He went down to the bar to look. I stayed in the chair and looked over the spines of the books I'd collected over the years when I was young, foolish, and hopeful, wanting to be a writer. What a fucking pathetic notion I'd held onto before the war and for a few weeks after it. I took out a volume of Franz Kafka. I wondered if he had been looking for a woman when his Tuberculosis finally murdered him. Or John Keats, or hell, even Jane Austen. I put the book back on the shelf, reached behind it and retrieved two dust covered pistol magazines for the 1911 Colt. Seven rounds in each. Perhaps overkill for looking for Jean, but I knew I would need it, and probably have to use it at some time or another in the near future. *A.B.C—always be carrying.* The phrase that I'd learnt in the Marines and never forgotten since. I'd probably end up using the thing on myself if things got bad enough, I joked in my head. Hardy fucking ha. I walked over to the cigar box, took out the pistol, slid in the magazine and cocked it. Made sure the safety was on and then pushed it into the small of my back, into the waist of my slacks. I tightened my belt, put on my blue check sport coat, placed the damp rag to my mouth again and slowly walked down the stairs after Charlie grasping at the wall as I went.

CHARLIE WAS STOOD behind the bar, a thick phone book opened in front of him, poking his dirty fingernail along the black type.

"Who the hell are you searching for, Charlie?" I said through the wet rag. He didn't hear. I sat down at the bar across from him like a patron and repeated myself.

"Who are you searching for?"

"I'm looking up Mickey Cohen. He's the King of Los Angeles. He'll give me a job. I'm sure of it," he grinned up at me.

"I really don't think he'd be in the directory, kid. Anyhow, people like him call you, you don't call them. Now slide that book over here, let me take a look at it."

He pushed it over towards me, sulkily.

"Did you at least eat the sunny side up eggs that I made for you?"

"I'm sorry. I'm not hungry. You go and eat them."

"Maybe, I will," he stomped dramatically upstairs, and I was glad to be alone in the darkness of the bar.

I checked under the S section for Spangler then remembered Jean didn't use her Ex-husband's name after the divorce. Spangler was her maiden name, so I checked under the Bs for Benner and quickly found him. Dexter Benner. Address and telephone number. He was living on North Alexandria Avenue. It wasn't far from where I was, but I went behind the bar and called a taxicab using the telephone attached to the wall next to a year-old cheesecake calendar. I ran the rag under the bar tap to get it good and wet. Wrote a note to Charlie telling him to stay here and watch the place. Put the rag to my mouth and sat down at a table by the window waiting for the taxicab, thinking I was that much closer to Jean now. I examined the maroon-going-brown smears on the bar rag and hoped Dexter would give me the information I needed without any persuasion. I doubted it. A man is probably the least forthcoming to help a guy when said guy has been fucking his ex-wife for years. Even at the best of times. Or the worst of times. The afternoon was nearly coming to an end already and I waited for the taxicab.

CHAPTER 5

THE TAXICAB PULLED up outside the house. A one-story duplex painted a moldy orange color. The lawn in worse shape than my lungs and three automobile tires piled in a stack by the front door, which had a black metal gate over it. Dead potted plants by the entrance steps. It all looked very depressing and I almost felt bad for Jean's ex-husband.

"This the right place, fella?" the driver asked.

"I hope so," I started to cough, and the driver eyeballed me in the rear-view mirror.

"You should get that cough checked out with a doctor, Pal. It might be the cancer. God forbidding, ya know. A buddy of mine smoked forty Luckies a day and caught it. The cancer, I mean. Smoking Luckies. Pretty shitty luck, if ya ask me, though. Anyhow, ya want me to wait? In case, it's not the right place, after all."

"No, it's okay. Thanks anyway."

"Okay then. Be healthy fella."

I tipped him good, got out and stood on the sidewalk until he drove off.

THE WOMAN WHO answered the door made me think of the advertisement for Kellogg's Pep vitamin pills: *"So the harder a wife works, the cuter she looks."*

I wondered if all advertisements lied? Kellogg's obviously did; that was for sure. Dexter had definitely picked Jean's opposite for his new wife. I really did start to feel sorry for the guy. He'd lost Jean, his daughter and ended up with a shitty duplex downtown and an already gone to shit new wife.

"Hello. Can I help you?" She was drying her hands on an

old, pink, stained apron she was wearing over a wrinkled, purple, polka dot dress.

"I'm here to see Mr. Benner. Is he home at the moment?"

She had the heavily lined face of a constant worrier or a heavy smoker. She looked me up and down, appraising me, the look of a woman who could've been a youthful forty-five or a haggard twenty-five. I didn't know which and wouldn't have placed a bet on it either way.

"Yes, he just got home from the plant and is sitting down for his dinner now," she opened the black gate and let me into the main hall as she spoke. The place smelt of boiled cabbage and pipe tobacco.

"Who should I say is here? Would you like me to take your jacket? You don't have a hat? Did you lose it?"

"No, no, it's okay. I'll not be stopping long. I'm an old friend of his. You can tell him that it's Scott Kelly."

Her demeanor automatically changed. Her pink lips made an ugly snarl and she started wiping her hands on her apron again. I took it she'd heard about me.

"Who is it, Sweetheart?" Dexter's voice came down the hall from the dining room and I started walking down towards that way with his new wife shouting after me.

"I think it's one of Jean's old boyfriends, Sweetheart."

By the way she said Jean's name I knew she hated her with the passion that all new wives had for the old wives.

I heard Dexter curse and the clatter of steel on cheap crockery as he set aside his plate. The squeal of a chair being pushed back.

"Now, what's the big idea here, coming to my—" He saw me coming through the dining room entrance and went slack jawed half-way through his sentence. He'd aged a lot since I'd seen him last and had lost a lot of weight, but his face was still that of a fat man. All nose and jowls, beady little eyes like a kid's marbles.

"Long time, no see, Dexter. How's the arm? All healed up, I hope."

"You've got some nerve coming here, to my house. You

fucking Irish degenerate!"

I ignored him and took a good gander around the place he called home. The dining room was as depressing as the front of the house. The cream wallpaper peeling from the walls and a large painting of a herd of elephants in a cheap frame hanging by a shoelace. 'Just Married' and 'Congratulations' cards strewn here and there. A vase of flowers in the center of the table, well past wilted. A pile of yellowing newspapers and magazines stacked on a shelf and a collection of empty milk cartons piled in the sink. What Jean had ever seen in this guy; I didn't know.

"Nice place you got here, Dex. It's... homely, like your new wife," I winked.

"Get the fuck outta my house," he shouted.

I could see by their reactions that the situation was sinking faster than the Lusitania. I'd never been a people person. I started to cough, tried to control it, got the damp rag up to my mouth and let rip. They both recoiled away from me and held each other tightly, next to a plate of sausages, mash potatoes and gravy. For the first time since I'd left the sanatorium, I realized I was hungry. I glanced at the blood on the rag, blasé and then held it up, showing it to them. I could feel trickles of cool sweat slide down my temples. I sat down heavily at the dining table and drunk from a glass of water, wiping away a lipstick stain on it before I put it to my mouth. Then I pulled the plate of food over to my side of the table, stuck a fork into a sausage and held it up, inspecting it as I spoke to them.

"Tuberculosis, it's a bitch, huh?"

Dexter untangled his wife's arms from his and motioned slowly to the hallway.

"It couldn't have happened to a nicer paddy. Lynn, Sweetheart, would you go down into the hall and call the police, please."

Before she'd even thought about moving, I'd taken out the Colt from the small of my back and had it shakily pointed at them. Waving it first at Dexter, then at his wife Lynn and back to Dexter again. It was heavier than I had remembered, my arm trembled from the weight.

"My ears work just fine, Dexter. Now sit. Sit down, both of you."

They both gasped, pulled faces and went back to holding each other.

Dexter looked as though he was about to cry. Lynn was made of sturdier stuff and stood there giving me the evil eyes.

"I said, sit down." I half barked; half spluttered the words.

They sat down. First Dexter and a few seconds later his wife followed. One either side of the dining table with myself at the head of it. It was like a family dinner.

"If this is about the private detectives again or anything else like that, I've not done anything wrong. I stopped all that a long time ago. The last... the last time."

"I'm looking for Jean," I said.

"What do you mean?"

I put the sausage into my mouth, bit into it and started to chew slowly. It didn't taste all that good, but I acted as though it did.

"You know full well what I mean, Dexter. Jean is missing and I want you to tell me where she is. She came here the evening she disappeared. To talk about money for your daughter. Child support payments," I said talking with my mouth full. Lynn cringed.

Dexter shook his head emphatically from side to side.

"No, no, no, I've already explained this to all the police officers and reporters that have come around here asking all the same questions. She never came here that night. Or any other night."

"I know you know where she is. And I'm not leaving here until you tell me. Let's stop wasting each other's time, Dexter."

"I haven't seen her for several weeks, maybe a couple of months. I send her the money for our daughter through a money transfer, through the mail. I don't know where she is, and I don't really care. She's probably run off again. She's probably in Mexico or Canada by now. Shirking her responsibilities as usual. Or running away from creditors most likely. Who knows with that woman? I think her sister is being melodramatic about the whole situation, reporting it all to the police and newspapers. It's probably another one of Jean's ruses to get more acting parts. She's run off to some motel somewhere and she'll be back in a week, probably."

"She wouldn't run away. She loved her life here in L.A"

"Maybe," he shrugged, "but maybe for all we know, she's running away from you, Kelly. Everyone knows about the beating you gave her the last time she tried to leave you. Two black eyes and a cracked tooth. You're a tough guy, Kelly, huh? Beating on women when they decide to leave your sorry ass."

"How about you shut your fucking mouth before I break your other arm?"

His eyes bulged, he wiped his mouth with the back of a trembling hand and continued. "The police are looking for a man, a lieutenant that gave her a bad beating and threatened her never to leave him or he'd kill her. They've got their information a little confused though, haven't they? They've been searching for a lieutenant named Scotty who was in the Air Force. You were in the Marines, weren't you, Kelly?"

"I never beat Jean. That's bullshit," I looked at his wife when I said it. I didn't know why.

"Well, everyone saw her face and that's what Jean told everyone anyway."

"I said, that's bullshit. You're lying. I'm going to put a bullet in your fucking head and then I'm going to put one in your wife's head. Now, I'm only going to ask one more time. Where can I find Jean?" I pulled back the hammer on the Colt and with the other hand forked a pile of mashed potatoes into my mouth. Dexter put his hands to his face and started to sob. His wife patted his back, there-there and turned her big fat lipped grimace towards me.

"He is telling the truth. He hasn't seen that woman's face in a long time. She never came here at all and I'm glad she is gone. I hope she never comes back. She was an awful woman and never loved Dexter at all. She used him, the same way she has used you. But you're too blinded by her to see it. I feel sorry for you because you're a fool, Mr. Kelly. She's really done a number on you, hasn't she? Now put the gun away because Dexter's daughter is upstairs sleeping, worried sick about her selfish mother, not knowing where she is. Now you've heard what we have to say, so get out of our house, before I really do call the police."

I didn't want to, but I believed them. They hadn't seen her. I wasn't sure of much, but I was sure of that. I put the fork back down on the plate and returned the Colt to the small of my back. Felt unsteady as I stood up from the table. My right eye ached. My shirt was damp. I had wasted a whole day with nothing to show for it and nothing to help me find Jean. No closer to her than I had been yesterday in the sanatorium. So much time squandered. Hours wasted. Fuck.

"Why'd you come here anyway?" moaned Dexter, his face still in his hands.

"You were the only one I could think of to ask. The tabloid newspapers said she'd been here," I said it low, almost a whisper. He took his face out of his hands and glared at me.

"How about asking all your wop and kike friends, huh?"

"What do you mean?" I asked, but he didn't answer, just covered his face with his hands again, sniveling. It was his new wife who answered;

"He means she spreads herself pretty thin, that woman. She's been bed hopping with Lord knows how many of those no-good, swarthy types. That's what he means."

"Mob guys?"

"Yes, your own friends. You foolish man."

Cowed. They had cowed me. I couldn't believe it. Dexter eyeballed me and let out a sarcastic, hurt little chuckle;

"You never really knew Jean at all. Did you? Go and ask your gangster pals about her and you'll know her a lot better. Jean was always a big black hole sucking all the men around her into it. Did you think she was only fucking you? You couldn't have been that naive, surely, a tough mick like you."

I stared at the painting of the elephants on the wall and counted backwards, trying to control my breathing. Cowed. Dexter continued;

"Do you actually think she really loved you, Kelly?"

"I know she loved me." As soon as I said it, I felt embarrassed. Weak. I didn't know why. They both laughed at me then. The cruel, mocking kind of laughter I'd not heard since I was ten years old, newly arrived in California.

"Jean never loved anybody. I don't think Jean loved anyone but herself. It's debatable she even loved our daughter," Dexter said, waving his hand at the ceiling. I felt small and ridiculous. Embarrassed. I thought about killing them both to salvage some kind of dignity from the situation. I would not be cowed like that. Who the fuck did they think they were? Who the fuck was I? I had my hand behind my back grasping the pistol with a sweaty grip, wanting to put a bullet in both of their ugly faces. I decided against it. It would only hamper my chances of finding Jean and Jean's daughter was upstairs after all.

"Thanks for the dinner," I said quietly.

I walked down the hall and out of the front door. After it had clicked shut, I heard Dexter shout belatedly; "Now get the fuck outta my house and go to hell."

He didn't realize that I'd already gone. I had a season ticket and front row seats.

CHAPTER 6

FROM DEXTER'S DEPRESSING home, I decided to start walking to Beverly Hills. I had nowhere else left to go. I'd been there a few times, it was a nice neighborhood, for sure. Home to the rich and famous and all that bullshit. I looked over my shoulder down the street for a taxicab or a kind face behind a windshield to thumb a ride from as I stumbled along. It would probably be a two hour walk to Anthony Cornero's mansion. I'd need a ride if I wanted to get there without coughing my lungs up on the concrete and dying at the side of the road in a ditch. I wished like hell I hadn't sold my Buick before I'd gone into the sanatorium. I took my time walking, shuffling my feet slowly, pretending to be taking a stroll. Stopping every five minutes to catch my breath and cough into the rag.

My thoughts kept jumping from Jean to the milk cartons in Dexter's kitchen sink. Milk cartons.

Cartons of milk.

A CARTON OF milk sat in front of a Mexican. The carton was bloody and so was the Mex. A tough amigo. He had been tied to a chair and beaten for two days straight. Sitting in his own crustified shit and piss and blood. He'd kept swollen, ruptured eye contact with me the whole time. Defiant and willful, refusing to drink the carton of milk in front of him. The mechanic's garage we were using was humid, enclosed and smelt worse than the war had. I was tired and wanted to go home to Jean. She was cooking steak for that night's dinner.

"Hey?! Hey Amigo?! My woman is cooking dinner for me tonight. Steak, potatoes, onions, gravy. I'm fucking starving, so drink the fucking milk will you. Let's get this shit over with.

Okay? You understand me? I want to go home already."

He stared at me; fish eyed. Black stuff oozed out of his nose and ears. Hard-headed bastard. I looked over at his friend, another spic. A dead spic. The dead friend was tied to a chair too, pantless, in soiled, bloody underpants, dead two days with a bullet hole through the front of the head and being eaten by bugs. I'd wondered how the bugs had even got inside the garage? All the windows were shut tight. It was another of life's little mysteries. The spic's dead buddy reeked. The kind of stench that sticks at the back of your throat. I had thought the whole situation excessive. I didn't like it. I'd told the living spic that, but he stared through me. A Zen Buddhist monk. The only way I knew he was still alive was by watching his chest rise and fall through the blue bowling shirt he was wearing.

A telephone rang on the mechanic's worktable. It made me jump, but the Mexican was motionless. Constant eye contact. I had to respect the man, he had guts by the barrelful. I went over to answer the phone knowing who it was before I picked up the receiver.

"Yeah?"

"It's me," Anthony Cornero.

"I know. How're you feeling? Are you feeling any better?"

"A little better. My stomach still fuckin' hurts, I can't eat anything fuckin' solid yet of course and I'm still stuck in this fuckin' bed. Doctors' orders. Did that wetback, spic, cunt drink the carton of milk, yet?"

"No. Not yet. He is resisting. Understandably."

"You need to be a little more persuasive, you were a fuckin' Marine for cryin' out loud. Why ain't he drinkin' it?"

"Probably, because it's got his partner's sliced off prick in it."

"Well, that's the idea, ain't it. I gotta make examples outta these kinda pricks. They came to my house, Scotty! To my fuckin' home!"

"It's been two days of beating this spic. He ain't going to drink that milk. I'm tired. I'll just finish it now."

"No, make him finish the carton of milk and then fuckin' finish him. Then and only then. Four in the gut and one in the head. Swing by the house later. I'll give you your salary and a nice little bonus."

"Right, okay. Understood."

"Ah, before I forget, what's the name of that restaurant you told me about? The one you took your girl, Jean to last month?"

"The Jap restaurant?"

"Yeah, that's the one. The one you said had all those little geisha girls and those little trees and shit. Barbara wants to take a few of her girlfriends there tonight. She loves all that oriental type of shit."

"It's called Motoyama's near the Chinese theater."

"Raw fish and rice. People eat that? Un-fuckin-believable. Anyway, I'll see you later tonight."

I hung up and walked over to the stubborn Mex, put my Colt to his blood caked stomach. He smiled at me with yellow teeth, nodded and I pulled the trigger two times and then capped it off with one in the head. Eye contact the whole time, even after he was dead. I was hungry, I wanted to go home to Jean, and thought the prick in the milk carton too excessive. Reminded me of something that the Japs would have done in Okinawa, but the Italians got to the top by being excessive, and the two Mexicans did have it coming, I supposed.

After the government closed down Anthony's floating casinos, he had been making moves in Baja, California, investing in things down there. Making waves. Maybe he'd skimmed too much cash or maybe he'd stepped on someone's toes, but nine days before, these same two spics had gone to Anthony's home in Beverly Hills. They'd knocked on the door and when he answered it, the ballsy spic had given Anthony a carton of milk and said, "here, Cornero, this is for you" shot him four times in the gut.

I didn't know what all the milk cartons were supposed to symbolize; I didn't ask. It was some wop versus spic thing. The Mexicans didn't finish the job properly and Anthony went into surgery at Cedars of Lebanon Hospital where doctors worked on him all through the night. As soon as he pulled through enough to gain consciousness and mutter a few words, the call had come to the bar and he had given me the job from his hospital bed; find those two wetbacks and keep them alive for further instructions. The further instructions had been the excessive bullshit with the carton of milk with a cut off prick floating around inside. If I had known it was going to be that much trouble and effort, I would have turned the whole job down flat.

IT WAS OVER a year since the milk cartons and I had heard talk that Anthony was planning on moving into Las Vegas again, partnering with Meyer Lansky on some project. He and his third wife Barbara still lived in the same large house in Beverly Hills and I knew he was the one person who could give me the information that I needed about Jean. Anthony was a killer and a brilliant businessman, but he also loved collecting gossip and always kept one ear to the street. People talked about little black books, but Anthony was *the* little black book. He knew everybody and everything. If anyone knew where I could find Jean or point me in the right direction, it was Anthony. My last hope to find Jean, otherwise I'd have to start muscling nervous movie extras and over-privileged Hollywood types that would likely call the cops and I knew nothing about that world or its inhabitants. I wouldn't even know where to start.

I had been stumbling along the road for what seemed like an eternity and it was well after dark before a clapped-out Ford Business Coupe finally submitted to my thumb in the beam of their headlights and clattered to a stop a few yards in front of me, kicking up grit and dust. I hobbled over to it and bent down, looking in at the driver. I saw the orange tip of a burning cigarette and the silhouette of a young woman.

"You looking for a ride?"

"Yeah, I'd be much obliged, Miss."

She leaned over the passenger seat, pushed open the door for me. It made a creaking noise and I saw in the streetlight that she was a Jap.

"You getting in or not?" her California accent much more pronounced than my own. I got in the Ford and slammed the door softly. Moving my pistol from my back into my sport coat side pocket as I did. It stuck out. I put my hand over the pocket and sat down properly into the seat. The Ford smelt good. A sweet perfumed fragrance that I didn't recognize and good tobacco. The change from the street air to the atmosphere inside the smoky automobile made me hack a few times. I brought the dried rag to my face and tried to clear my system out.

"You sick, Mister?"

I finished hacking and wiped my mouth.

"Yeah, consumption. Tuberculosis."

She turned to look at me carefully and I saw she was a knockout. Caramel skinned and almond eyed. Dark hair pushed into a careless bun on top of her head, away from her long smooth neck like she'd just finished a ballet rehearsal. She inhaled long on her cigarette, still looking at me and then exhaled the smoke out of a gap at the top of her window. She was wearing a tight, white blouse and a tighter brown skirt that made her look much older than the very early twenties, I guessed she was. The whole getup really displayed how she had a ripened woman's body. She was perfect in all the right places. All eyes, lips, breasts, and legs. I could almost forget that I even had consumption. Then I thought of Jean.

"You want me to get out?" I asked.

"Why?"

"Because I said I have consumption. Tuberculosis. People usually get worried about it."

She shrugged. "It's okay, I suppose. You can't catch consumption by breathing the same air, I think. I'd only get it if you coughed in my face. Are you going to cough in my face?"

"Never on the first date," I grinned.

"Where do you wanna go? The hospital?" she smiled with lips that were red and plump like rose petals.

"No, I've already escaped from there. I want to go to Beverly Hills."

She laughed *ha-ha* and nodded her head in an understanding bow, took a long drag on her cigarette and smiled again with those lips.

"Okay, Mister, it's your funeral."

"I hope I'm not too late for it."

I laughed a little at that and she laughed that I had laughed at my own joke. She put the old Ford into drive and pulled into a steady stream of loose traffic. We didn't talk for a little while and then when it had started to seem like an awkward silence, we started a tentative conversation again.

"So, what's your name?" she asked.

"I'm Scott. And you?"

"Yumiko. But my friends call me Yumi."

"Okay, nice to meet you, Yumi."

"I said, my friends call me Yumi," she laughed again, it was a husky and sensuous sound like the tobacco smoke that rippled through the air around me. It definitely gave me something. She unwound her window and threw her cigarette butt out, wound the window back up again.

"Was the smoke bothering your breathing?"

"No, not at all," I lied.

"So, why are you going to Beverly Hills, Scott?"

"I'm looking for someone, a woman. Someone very important to me."

"Your sweetheart?"

"Yeah, I guess so. I've not called her that before, but I guess, yeah, she is my sweetheart."

"She lives in Beverly Hills? She must be pretty wealthy."

"She doesn't live there. She lives in Wilshire, actually."

"Why are you looking for her in Beverly Hills then? I'm sorry. Am I asking too many questions? Do you mind?"

"No, not at all. It's your automobile, after all. Ask all the questions you want." I shrugged and watched the passing headlights of other automobiles flash across her face.

"So, then?" she shrugged, mirroring me.

"She's gone missing and I'm trying to find her. Someone I know in Beverly Hills, an associate of mine, might know where she has gone to," I started to cough into the rag again. The inside of the car was very dark, but I knew it was a heavy hemorrhage in the rag this time. Felt it. It was getting worse. I felt like I was going to pass out again. I sat wheezing heavily, my throat rattling as I gazed out at the darkness and light of Los Angeles. After a while she spoke.

"That sounds so sad, Scott. I'm really sorry for your situation."

I wasn't sure if she was talking about searching for Jean or my cough. It was probably both. I changed the topic.

"Where are you going to this evening, Yumi?" I rasped.

"I volunteer sometimes at a place called JUGS. I'm going there tonight to help them prepare for a Halloween dance event."

"JUGS? What's that? Like a bar or club? I've not heard of it before."

"Just Us Girls. It's a Nisei youth club for girls, hence the name. We started it during the time when we were in the confinements. You know the camps during the war? Anyway, we continued the clubs after to help a lot of the younger Nisei like myself. It's been difficult for a lot of us the last few years, so it gives all the girls a chance to let their hair down and have a little fun. Dance. Make friends. Meet guys. That kind of thing. It's a way to take something good out of the confinements."

"Yeah, I'm sorry about that. The confinements and resettlements. It always seemed a dirty shame to me. Americans are Americans, after all. Everyone's an immigrant in this country. Sure, I was pissed after Pearl Harbor, everyone was. I fought in Okinawa, but I never hated the Japs. It was war, nothing personal. Just another job. I always respected them. They were tough and persistent, one and all."

She smiled at that, "you're nice to say that, Scott. Anyways, what's she like? Your sweetheart?"

"She's an amazing woman."

"Wow, that sounds like a ringing endorsement. So, how is she amazing, Scott?"

"Well, she's beautiful, stunning actually and she was the

74

only one there for me when I became sick. She cares about me a lot. She makes me feel good. You know? All the usual Hallmark card kind of sentiment." I cringed at my honesty.

"How does she make you feel good?"

"No one's ever asked me that before."

"I'm an original kinda gal, Scott."

"You're really interested, huh?"

"Maybe, I'm doing my homework on how to be a good little wifey."

"I'm sure you don't need to do any homework," I grinned. She grinned back and giggled.

"Well, I don't know. She makes me feel, happy, I guess. Maybe, that sounds soft, like I said, I don't know what to say."

She took another cigarette from the box on the dashboard and lit it, wound down her window a crack and blew the smoke out.

"No offense intended, Scott, and I know I don't know you very well. But it sounds as though you're not in love with her, you're in love with the way she makes you feel. Is that why you're looking for her, to get those feelings back? To make yourself seem worthwhile? Your life?"

"Woah. What the fuck are you? A psychiatrist?"

"No, but I read a lot, study a lot. Anyways, I'm sorry if I made you upset. It was wrong of me to say it so bluntly, after all, I only just met you. It was foolish. I apologize, Scott."

"No, it's okay. I'm sorry if I was rude just now. I wasn't expecting to be psychoanalyzed."

"It's okay, I've heard much worse, believe me."

I changed the subject again. "Do have a sweetheart, Yumi?" She giggled, shy little schoolgirl style.

"No, to be honest, I'm too American for a lot of Japanese guys. They don't like it so much, I think."

"Yeah, you're pretty straight-talking for a Japanese woman. Maybe, too straight-talking for any kind of woman."

She giggled again, "I like American guys, if I'm honest about it. I was going steady with a wonderful man; his name was Henry. I would have married him, but when America joined in the war with Europe, he was drafted."

"What happened? He wasn't the same man when he came back?"

"No, not that. I wish it *were* that. He didn't come back at all. I never saw him again."

"I'm sorry to hear that, Yumi."

"It's okay, it took me a long time to find peace, but I'd like to find someone like him again. A kind, loyal, romantic man. I heard a rumor that there are some still out there."

"If you don't mind me saying, I'm sure there's a bunch of guys lining up for a girl like you."

That giggle again and then we drove in silence the rest of the way.

BEVERLY HILLS HADN'T changed much since the last time I was there. I saw Benny Siegel's woman's house and it hadn't changed either. The white picket fence I'd used to rest the .30 caliber Carbine on was still there. As were the large bay windows I'd watched Benny read the Los Angeles Times for the last time in. I was sure Benny had looked up and seen me there in the darkness before I'd pulled the trigger. He'd probably never expected I'd be the one to finish his story. That's the way it always goes.

When we got to Anthony's street, I pointed out his house and Yumi pulled over to the curb outside.

"That's a nice-looking house. Your friend must be somebody pretty influential."

"Yeah, I hope he is."

"Well, it's been a short, but happy road trip with you. I hope you find your sweetheart, Scott."

I bent down, leaned into the passenger's side window after I got out and looked at her in the streetlight coming through the windshield. She was even more stunning than at first thought.

"I really appreciate your kindness, Yumi. You're a really swell girl," I dropped a wad of bills onto the passenger seat. "That's for gasoline."

"There's over a hundred dollars here," she frowned.

"Buy yourself something nice, you certainly earned it, you might have saved my life this evening by picking me up."

She tried to push the wad back out the window towards me, "I can't accept this, Scott."

"Please," I said, closing her hand over the bills. She sunk back into her seat, placed another cigarette in her lips and said, "If you don't find your sweetheart and when you cure your consumption, look me up sometime. I'll be at the JUGS club. You should come for a dance. It'll be fun. I can try and psychoanalyze you again."

Her eyes were shining, it took a lot of my willpower not to get back into the old Ford and drive off with her.

"Maybe I will," I said and winked. She winked back and drove away, playing 'Shave and a Haircut' on the horn. I felt my stomach suddenly drop, I thought about Jean.

EVEN IN THE darkness Anthony's house still looked ridiculously pretty. Maybe more so all lit up in the darkness. A lot of mob guys joked about it behind his back; said it wasn't befitting a gangster. They had dubbed it 'The Dolls House'. But what I had known that they didn't was the place was picked and decorated by Anthony's third wife Barbara, as part of the bargain for her to get hitched with him. He may have been a tough guy, but Barbara wore the pants in that relationship.

The place was a large mansion built in the style of a French chateau, the stone walls painted the brightest white with all the edges and skirtings painted a tone of baby blue. Two large multicolored flower gardens stretched from the sidewalk all the way down to their front windows either side of the pathway to the front door. If Dexter was one side of a coin, Anthony was the other. He had a gorgeous actress wife, half his age, a big house, a lot of money in the bank and a heap of investments in all the right places. He was the poster boy for American Capitalism and a rag to riches story ripped straight from a

Horatio Alger novel. He'd been out in Vegas building things up before Benny Siegel had even thought about going out there and stealing his idea. I'd met Barbara a few times, she was often on the verge of being drunk and overtly flirtatious. I liked her a lot. She had what people called "moxie". I hadn't met the second wife because the marriage was over before introductions were even done. His first wife Dorothy was a gorgeous babe. But that had gone south with a bad divorce and Dorothy ended up crippled in a bad automobile accident while being chased by another automobile. Anthony had been driving that other automobile. It wasn't something that was ever talked about. Anthony was the biggest fool for beautiful women. Even more so than myself, maybe.

I knocked on the white pristine door and Barbara answered a few moments later, drinking champagne and wearing a black, silk kimono, her long blond hair hanging down in ripples to the milky, freckled cleavage of her large breasts, nipples pressing through the fabric. She shrieked with joy when she saw me and jumped up and down like a teenage girl. It was difficult to know where to look.

"Scotty! Oh, Scotty! Where ya been? I haven't seen ya in such a long while."

"Hello Barbara. You haven't changed at all. You still look as pretty as ever."

"Oh Scotty, ya always were a smooth operator. I could just eat ya all up. I'll go and get Tony. Come in, come in, please."

"Is he in bed? I'm sorry if it's late. I forgot to wind my wristwatch, so I'm not sure what time it is."

"No, don't be sorry," she looked at the gold and diamond wristwatch hanging loosely from her small wrist.

"It's only nine thirty-five and Tony is in his office upstairs as per usual. He is always in that office. Such a dullard, I assure you." She sipped seductively from the champagne glass and then bellowed up the stairs;

"Tony! Anthony! Scotty's here."

She looked back at me and put her palm against my chest, above my heart. "Why did ya lose so much weight, Scotty? Ya used to be so big and strong. Ya look like a sudden gust of wind would blow ya away now. You on some kind of a diet or something like that? I'm on a diet myself."

"I was sick. In the hospital," I said.

"Oh no, I'm real sorry to hear that, Scotty. Nothing too bad, I hope." She gulped the rest of the champagne and then shook the empty glass at me, skipped off deeper into the house, bored by my company already.

Anthony came thumping down the stairs, as I looked around the hall and at the black and white photographs on the wall. Anthony and Joe DiMaggio. Anthony standing in front of the gambling ship Johanna Smith before it was raided by the government. Anthony and George Raft. Anthony, Benny Siegel and Meyer Lansky sitting at a restaurant table, drinking. Anthony and Mickey Cohen pointing at each other and playing up to the camera. Anthony pulling a boxing pose with Jack Dempsey. I always looked at the same photographs every time I was there. Awkward in other people's homes, it seemed like the best thing to do.

"Well, look who ain't dead yet," Tony came over and embraced me. Taking the breath out of my lungs with a bear hug. I struggled to stifle a hack.

"The fuckin' Marine! Come on up to the office," he patted me on the shoulder and the small of my back a few times as we walked up the red carpeted stairs. It was done as a friendly gesture, but I knew he was checking to see if I was carrying or not.

"Hey Babs, get us some drinks will ya?" he shouted down.

"Get em, yourself, Tony. I'm not ya servant, ya know?" she shouted up.

"Look at that, will ya. Almost on my third divorce and I only just turned fifty. Third times the charm, right? You tell me, you're the Irishman. Talking of drinks, who's looking after the bar nowadays? I drove past it the other day and all the lights were on. I'd thought you would've closed it down. You sell the place?"

"That kid, Charlie, the one who served under me in the

Marines is looking after it for a while."

"That fuckin' kid who wants to be a button man?"

"Yeah, that's the one."

"Tell him to clean the windows occasionally. The place is starting to look like a shit hole dive."

I nodded and Tony chuckled heartedly.

HIS OFFICE WAS how it had always been. A large dark wood Art Deco desk, blood red chesterfield furniture, more black and white, framed photographs, and clouds of grey cigar smoke. He sat down behind his desk and motioned me into the opposite chair.

"It's good to see you again, I mean it's fuckin' great to see you, last I heard, you had the consumption or plague or something. You look like shit, but it's good to see you outta the hospital, finally healthy and well. I always say you can't keep a good mutt down. Am I right or am I fuckin' right?"

I started hacking on cue, another large, dark red hemorrhage soaked into the rag.

"Speak of the devil and he shall appear," I croaked, showing him the scrunched up, clotted fabric in my hand.

"Jesus fuckin' Christ, Scotty," he yanked out a silk handkerchief from a pocket in his black slacks and balled it into his lower face around his mouth and nose.

"I don't need a pistol to work nowadays, all I need to do is cough on people," I tried to smile.

"Are you fuckin' joking with me? You come to my fuckin' house like that? We are very old and dear friends, Scotty, and no offense, but are you fucking contagious? Jesus fuckin' Christ what were you thinkin'? Are you contagious?"

"Not unless I sneeze on you or cough in your face. It's okay from this distance, Anthony. Don't worry about it."

"Don't fuckin' worry about it, he says. I'm still getting over four bullets in the gizzard. You forget about that?"

"The milk carton assassination attempt. How could I forget?"

"I still can't eat anything spicy; the doctor says it'll kill me. Forget about bullets, force feed me a chili pepper. Shit fortuna or what?" he said holding the handkerchief to his face and rubbing his stomach with his free hand.

"One day you're shitting gold and the next your shitting blood," I said frowning at the stains on the rag.

"You're shitting fuckin' blood?" Tony pushed his chair back.

"No, it was just an expression."

"What expression?"

"Mine. Forget about it."

"Next you'll be telling me you got the leprosy. You don't do ya?"

We both chuckled, but his chuckle was the nervous hardy ha-ha kind of laugh and he still hadn't removed the handkerchief from his mouth and nose.

"I can see you're in a pretty bad fuckin' shape, Scotty, and I'm reckoning you checked yourself outta the sanatorium or paid someone off, so you could leave, am I right? So, let's cut out the bullshit and get to the heart of the matter. You're here about Jean, right? I seen the newspapers."

"That's right," I said, folding the rag and putting it back in my jacket pocket.

"I just wanna say I never fucked that broad, Scotty. Everyone knew she was your girl. Us Italians, we got rules. Never fuck another man's woman and you're a dear friend of mine. Anyhow, you know I go for the blondes."

"Yeah, I know all that. What I need to know is where she's at. I heard she was seen with some of the guys and I need to know where she might be now."

He leaned back deeply into the Chesterfield behind his desk and finally removed the handkerchief from his wide pale face, threw it towards a closet. Took an old half smoked cigar out of the desk ashtray and relit it, using a solid gold lighter. Looked at me and raised his big eyebrows.

"Who told ya that?"

"An old buddy, in The Department." I lied. He raised his

eyebrows again and blew a smoke ring.

"I thought all your old cop contacts withdrew their services after that beach house job for Benny. That was a fuckin' mess. Talk about bad publicity, huh?"

My heart started pulsing inside my rib cage. Prickly heat ran up my spine and over the flesh of my face. Cold sweat. I started wheezing again. Heavily.

"Hey, Scotty! Scotty! You okay?"

I tried to focus on something solid. My right eye ached. I didn't want to pass out again. Didn't want any more relapses into the fadeout. That old theater of memory. That old child's nursery rhyme being hummed by a child. Mother and daughter, jumping hand in hand. They leapt hand in hand over and over again. The Daughter screaming for her daddy. Daddy.

"Scott! Marine! Snap outta it, Son," Anthony leaned his heavy mass over the desk, gave me a quick slap on the top of my scalp and then wiped his hand on his shirt. I focused on Anthony face. Strong, square and milky with large contrasting eyebrows and a big Roman nose. I counted. Tried to breathe. I fumbled for my rag and breathed into it. Smelling dried blood. That menstruation scent. Anthony took out a bottle of whisky from a desk draw, two glasses and poured them both. He passed one over to me and I took it with a trembling hand, drank it quickly.

"You straightened out now?"

I nodded.

"I know where you went. Just now, you went somewhere, right? I get like that myself sometimes. We've done so much awful shit to get where we are, God won't let us fuckin' forget it. Sometimes, I'll be doing something like sitting at a red light in traffic, something will make me remember and then I'm back there. It's like watching something in the theater, but it's your life. I don't know. Maybe, I'm getting too fuckin' old. Getting squirrelly in my old age." I nodded at him and he nodded back. A shared understanding of what it was like to have a portion of Hell inside your head at all times of the day.

"Davy," he said as he poured me another drink.

"Davy?"

"Yeah, Davy. The broad has been hanging around with Davy these days."

"Davy Ogul?"

"Davy fuckin' Ogul, the fat prick. That was partly why I mentioned the beach house thing before. You know you fractured his skull, nearly pistol whipped him to death that day. He talks with a slur now. The fat fuck sounds like a paddy drunkard all the time when he talks. No offence."

"Jean is with him?" I couldn't believe it.

"That's what I heard. I'm sorry to say it to you, but she's been running around with him a lot and for a while too."

I didn't know what to say. I didn't know why Jean would have gone with a guy as low as Davy. There must have been a reason for it. A good reason.

"What is Jean doing with a scumbag like Davy?"

Anthony didn't answer, he shrugged and raised his eyebrows again.

"Where's Davy now?" I asked.

"You see, this is where things become very problematic."

"Anthony, If Jean is with Davy, I want to meet them right now. I want to see her, right away."

"Like I said, it's problematic."

"Anthony. We have been friends a long time now. I've done a lot of favors for you in the past and I've never asked anything from you in return. With all due respect, I'm not asking you here."

"Okay, okay, let me get to it, will ya? Davy is under indictment for conspiracy."

"And?"

"He's gone on the lamb. Your girl Jean disappeared on the 7th the newspapers said and DavyI know probably followed her. Disappeared around the 7th as well. It's not a coincidence."

"So, where the fuck are they?"

"They're in Palm Springs, last I heard it. In a hotel or motel or who the fuck knows where?"

"Palm Springs? Jean went to Palm Springs with fucking

Davy? Now I know something is wrong. She wouldn't have gone there with him. She wouldn't have gone there with him of her own free will."

He shrugged again.

"You got an address?" I asked.

"No, that I don't have."

"Get it for me."

"Look, Scotty, I wanna help you, but my hands are tied here. The only person who knows where he is, ain't going to tell you. Everyone knows you hate Davy's guts and wanted to snuff him."

"Tell me who they are, and I'll get the address myself."

"Like I said, it's problematic."

"How?"

"It's problematic, because like I been saying, Davy Ogul is under indictment and he is on the lamb. You know what Davy is like, he's a slippery fuckin' fat snake. Knew he was going to get snuffed out to stop him from turning canary, so he came up with the genius idea of stealing three hundred thousand dollars' worth of brown and stashing it with three of his LAPD contacts. Then lets it be known that if he catches any bullets and doesn't make it across the border to Mexico, the chance of the brown returning to its rightful owners dies with him."

"So, torture the prick and find out the names of the dirty cops."

"I don't know if you've noticed or not, but our people are currently at war with the LAPD, maybe no one told you up there in the sanatorium. We can't touch any of the cops cos' it'd be very bad for business. Hell, it'd be suicide for all of us. They'd probably call out the National fuckin' Guard. I gotta give it to Davy though, it is a genius fuckin' plan. He's protected from the top now. The word is out; no one is to hurt Davy Ogul, by punishment of death themselves. When he finally gets to Mexico and when we get back our brown, then that might be a different thing altogether though."

"I don't give a shit about the junk. I want to know the fucking address he is at, Anthony. Now!"

"I've known you for four long years and you still call me Anthony. Not Tony. Not one time. Why is that? I wonder sometimes. You sound like my mother, God rest her soul."

He picked up the black telephone next to him on the desk and dialed a number. Waited.

"It's Tony... Tony Cornero... Yeah, that's right... Okay, put him on..." I watched a bead of perspiration slowly roll down the side of his face, under his chin and fall onto the desk when he started talking again;

"Yeah... I'm good... Look, this isn't a social call. I've got the Marine sat here with me now... in my house... he's looking for Davy and wants an address... yeah, I'll put him on the line..."

He passed me the receiver. I took it and put it to my ear. It was warm and damp.

"Hello?" I said.

There was a nasal breathing I had heard on the phone a couple of years before.

"Scott Kelly, Boychik. It's been too long since our last phone call. What do ya say, what do ya know?"

Mickey Cohen.

"I'm doing alright, Mickey. And you?"

"Not so great. I've got the LAPD and Jack Dragna so far up my tuchas, I'm fuckin' constipated over here."

"That's unfortunate, Mickey."

"The cops are trying to murder me too. They shot me outside Sherry's! The cops! That fuckin' degenerate police chief Parker wants me dead. How about that for unfortunate? And to top it all off they're tryin' to bust me on the same shit they got Al fuckin' Capone on. Ya believe this bullshit?"

"You're still alive. Sounds pretty fortunate to me."

"Heavy is the head that wears the crown."

"Mickey, I want the address of where Davy is holed up."

"Always straight to business, no schmoozing. No, 'how's the weather, Mickey?' bullshit. I always liked that about you, Scott. You did me a solid with Benny, so I'll do a favor for you. But on the condition that you don't hurt a hair on Davy's head. And yeah, I know Davy's bald, it was a figure of speech.

Anyway, I know you and Davy don't exactly like each other, because of that business before. Ya put him in the hospital for over a fuckin' month and he talks all fucked up now, so I wanna know what ya wanna see him about first?"

"I'm looking for someone and I think she is with him."

"She? This is all about a woman!? Oy! Why ain't I surprised?"

"Her name's Jean Spangler."

"The broad from the newspapers? Half of California is looking for her! Jesus fuckin' Christ. That's a problem I need like I need another hole in my head. Farkakte! Okay, listen here, I'll give ya the address, but remember that nothing bad is to happen to the boychik. We were little pishers, grew up together and he's kidnapped my horse, and that piece of shit gonef is the only one who can get it back from those dirty cops for me. You understand me, Scott? Nothing bad happens to Davy. Not so much as a broken fingernail. That fucked up shit with you both is in the past and buried with Benny now. That's over with. You just meet Davy and politely schmooze about the broad and that's it. Did I say that we grew up together? Davy and me? He's like a brother to me. If, he gets to Mexico and only after I get my investment back, then maybe I'll call you again. But not a fuckin' minute before. You understand? I wanna hear you say you understand."

"I understand." I said.

"Say the past is the past, Mickey."

"The past is the past, Mickey."

"I owe you a mitzve Marine, so I'll play ball, help you out, this once. L.A belongs to me, partly because of you. Nobody can say Mickey Cohen doesn't repay a favor. Nobody can say Mickey Cohen is a welcher."

"Thank you, Mickey."

"Ya know, I still don't know how ya got him right in the eye? That was some old testament-like retribution shit. A bullet through the fuckin' eye. That guy and his fuckin' casino, thinking he was going to be the next Errol Flynn... Anyhow, go to Palm Springs, find the broad, get the broad back, get laid and don't fuck with my business and don't fuck with Davy otherwise things will become difficult for you and I mean the permanent kind of difficult."

"I said I understand, Mickey."

My right eye ached. He gave me the address, I noted it down using a pen and paper on the desk, hung up the phone and looked at Anthony's sweaty pale face.

"I'm going to Palm Springs," I said.

"I really think this is a bad idea. You and Davy already fuckin' hate each other and now there's Jean's involvement. You got the consumption. I don't like it, Scotty. I think it's going to end badly for you."

I looked him in the eye and said, "Anthony you of all people know how difficult it is to let a woman go."

His eyes glazed over for a minute and he went somewhere in his mind. One of the repeat movie showings he said he knew about, "I know that chasing a woman that wants to run away from you is a crippling thing and only ends up in a pile of shit for all parties involved. I can't change your mind and you look like a dead man right now, Scotty, It's late, stay in the guest room here tonight and I'll get my driver to take you to Palm Springs early tomorrow morning, after you've had breakfast. I'll get Babs to make ya some pancakes or something. How's that sound to ya?"

"Thank you, for everything, Anthony."

"Don't mention it. Just try not to breathe all over everything in my house. We'll have to fuckin' burn everything after you leave tomorrow. Am I right or am I fuckin' right?"

"Again, I appreciate your help."

"Go and get some shut eye, ya crazy fuckin' mad dog mick."

I went down the hall into a garishly bright red guest room, locked the door, undressed, and collapsed onto the large, white, four poster bed, into an exhausted unconsciousness.

CHAPTER 7

I HAD GONE veering along these streets and roads for a long time, for too many times.

My eyes were always closed, the sun shone through my eyelids burning shapes and for a moment everything was dark with white shadows.

A place like Purgatory.

Before I'd left the house early that morning, I'd glimpsed, momentarily the smoky image of my daughter and Beth in the kitchen making pancakes. Christmas of '46. My daughter had loved pancakes. She was wearing a paper crown on her head and braids in her hair.

In the automobile it wasn't Christmas, 1946.

It was June 1947. Jean still asleep upstairs in my bed wrapped in white sheets her hair spread over the pillows like ocean water on sand.

Then that stink of stale sweat and unwashed skin again. Heavy, labored breath again. The smooth clicking of tires on gritty lanes like dogs' claws on concrete. Creaking leather seats.

I could hear the ocean far off and Billie Holiday singing on the Motorola. A song called 'Gloomy Sunday'.

Davy Olga shook me awake. Beads of perspiration leaking from his upper lip like rainwater. He ate a candy bar. His lips slapped together obscenely, two fat cripples fucking. He sucked fat, pale fingers. He held the steering wheel with one bloated hand, removed his gaze from the road to roll his greasy moon face to squint at me. His voice moist spitting damp words. Stabbed his finger at me when he spoke.

Wake the fuck up! We're almost at the beach house, Soldier Boy, he said.

I woke up from life into something else.

The union delegate guy and his son are there, he said.

Panting, sneering. Yellow teeth and sickly-sweet breath.

In the house, he said.

Flakes of skin fell from his scalp like Christmas Day snowflakes, sprinkled on his meaty shoulders and down the cushion of the seat.

It's only them. I know, cos I been watching the place. Sure, I been watching the place good, he said.

Do em', ya gotta do em' both, he said.

Slapped his lips together as he talked. High pitch sniggered.

'Gloomy Sunday'. Billie Holiday sang so slowly on the Motorola.

This nigga's a fuckin' dyke, I heard, he said.

We'll go and get a steak and a couple of whores after to celebrate, he said.

I wanted to flee that automobile. I knew where it was going. It was going where it had always gone. Where it had always been. Journeys end. I was going home.

THE FAMILY HOME. The house grew and expanded in the windshield. A Cape Cod style, one floor beach house painted a sunset-bloody-red with a garage on the side. A veranda with a table and chairs out on the front. Large windows with an ocean view. All alone at the bottom of a sandy lane with a view of the blue Pacific Ocean. A family home. A house for a family.

A young man was out on the drive, fixing a motorcycle. The garage door was open, a blue truck parked inside.

Davy Olga licked his liver-colored lips. Twisted his neck towards me and looked. His eyes like drops of oil, smirked. He winked.

Make em' dead! The union delegate and his grease monkey son, he said and his eyes like drops of oil glistened like the morning sun on the ocean. Davy chewed on another candy bar; dribble ran down his flabby chin like phlegmy blood.

THE CAR STOPPED. I stepped out of the automobile. I had been there so many times before, it was like coming home. The sound of the ocean. Home.

THE SAND WHITE and soft between my toes. Five years old and in Kerry, Ireland. The air smelt like I'd always been there. And I had always been there. Full circle.

EVERYTHING SO DAMN white and the sky baby blue. The sun yellow on my skin and on the frothy surf and in the young man's blond hair.

Birds sang so slowly.

I strolled over to the young man; he was bent down over the motorcycle. His fingers blackened with grease and oil. My footsteps scraped over the gritty pathway.

I said hello, I was from the union and there to speak to his father.

He wiped his hand on the front of his white T-shirt, the smear of oil was a blood stain there. He shook my hand. He smiled. His teeth were very white. He had an oil smudge on his forehead and then it was a bullet hole. He wiped his hands again on a rag.

Sure, Mister. He's in the kitchen eating his lunch, you might as well come through the garage and join us for a bite to eat too, he said.

Not a young man, but a young, good-looking kid. Thinking about riding his motorcycle over sun warmed lanes in summertime, getting laid with cute college girls and getting drunk to celebrate being young and healthy. He reminded me a lot of myself before the war. As he led me into the garage, I put the silenced pistol to the back of his head and pulled the trigger.

It wasn't a war for a Kerry boy, my mother had said.

The pistol made a *thwump* noise. The grey concrete floor bled red and the boy still smiled with very white teeth. There was a carpenter's bench with a half made wooden, bird house on it. Particles of sawdust and sand on the floor. I shot the boy again in the back, above the heart. There was a red door to the right rear of the garage, I stepped over the body and I let myself in.

IT WAS A house for a family. A family home. I could smell warm, baked bread and the mist of the ocean. I could hear the soft hum of cheerful conversation as the union delegate came into my view. He was cutting a large, warm loaf of bread at a stone breakfast bar in the kitchen. His pretty wife wearing a blue cotton dress and braiding their pretty daughter's long, blonde hair. The little girl sat on a red leather stool kicking her legs back and forth happily. Humming and singing to herself; *Waltzing Matilda*… About the same age as my daughter. She looked the same as my daughter.

The guy and son are there, Davy had said.

It's only them. I know cos' I been watching the place. Sure, I been watching the place, Davy had said.

The family startled in unison when they noticed me stood in the doorway. The man held my eyes. I held the pistol. He saw my face. The wife saw my face. The daughter saw my face. The bread knife halfway through the loaf of bread and the son already dead in the garage, his forehead blossomed open like a flower wilted in a vase. My right eye ached. The woman said her husband's name, she caressed her daughter's hair. They looked at me, they looked at the pistol in my fist, a wild animal was in the house. The wife said her husband's name again. The husband looked at the pistol and then at my face. Their son already dead in the garage. Too late.

PAST LAST CALL at the bar and it was time to close up for the night.

SO BRIGHT, it looked like a star going supernova…

THE WIFE SAID her husband's name again. Her voice was very calm.

I shot the man through the face first and he disappeared from my view, behind the breakfast bar.

The wife screamed and grasped her daughter's hands very tightly. The daughter screamed *Daddy! Daddy! Daddy!*

They held hands and I told them I was sorry; they weren't supposed to be there.

MOTHER AND CHILD, leapt hand in hand…

THE MOTHER WRAPPED her daughter in her arms keeping her safe and blocking the child from pain and sorrow, but I shot the mother in the back. She collapsed at the little girl's bare feet. She was wearing a long cotton dress. It was blue. Blood soaked into the fabric and spread. I shot the mother again in the heart when she mouthed something to the child from the floor.

The little girl screamed *Daddy!*

The Pacific Ocean roared in my ears.

Birds sang so slowly, I told the little girl that she wasn't supposed to be there, but she couldn't understand what I was saying. She only kept saying Daddy and wailing and crying. I wanted to take her in my arms and protect her, but I didn't. I shot her twice in the chest. She died underneath the breakfast bar in her family home next to her dead mother. The little girl was so hard to do and as I left the house, I thought I heard her humming that child's nursery rhyme. But it was just the smell of bread, blood, and shit in the air of the kitchen as I slammed the door.

Fire ants were in my chest, eating me from the inside out. I walked down the beach and up to the surf. The ocean was a turquoise blue and the water ran up the grains of sand and over the toe caps of my shoes.

The sand that was white and soft between my toes, when I was five years old and in Kerry, Ireland. I looked around for my father, he'd been searching in the watery sand for mussels and cockles, but now he was dead, and he wasn't there.

Davy drove down to the house and yelled at me from the automobile.

What the fuck are ya doin'? Let's get outta here, he said.

He waddled around the automobile to me, his bald head shining in the white sun, as I walked up the beach towards him.

What the fuck's wrong with ya? he said.

His face bright, all turned up at the edges. He was joyful and I didn't know why.

There was a fucking woman and a little girl in there, I said. My voice cracked and broke.

So what, Soldier Boy? Who gives a fuck anyway? Ya gonna start sniveling bout it? He said and he smirked.

He turned around and walked back to the automobile.

My pistol *clicked, clicked, clicked.*

I brought down the butt of the pistol on the back of his head again and again. I wanted to split that fat fucking head open like a watermelon, like an egg. I brought down the pistol on his head again and again and again.

Crack! Crack! Crack!

Fire ants were in my chest, eating me from the inside out.

CRACK! CRACK! CRACK!

I was on the floor of the guest room. A white sheet tangled in my arms. Hacking and suffocating. I couldn't breathe. Drowning in my own lungs. That woman's menstruation taste in my mouth again. Jean had been gone eight days. Holed up with Davy in Palm Springs for eight fucking days. I coughed and hemorrhaged blood again.

Crack! Crack! Crack!

"Scotty, Darling, are ya alright?" Barbara was knocking at the guest room door. My ears rang loudly, but I could hear two bodies out there moving around softly and whispering.

"Unlock the door, Tony, he needs help."

"Don't fuckin' go in there, Barbara. I like the guy, but he is having a fuckin' seizure or something. Consumption's like the fuckin' plague. We'll both be in the sanatorium by Friday for the next six months if he coughs on us even once. Ya wanna risk that? Cos' I don't.'"

My breath was a deeper, thicker death rattle now and it took all my effort to crawl to my feet and to the door. I saw a man in a mirror. A tall and malnourished man. Bones and skin. Wearing a white vest that was stained heavily with maroon patches, he didn't have much time left. Or he'd really died on that hill in Okinawa years ago and this was a corpse's daydream. The breath came out of my mouth wet, heavy and thick.

I rested my head against the dark oak door and spoke through it;

"Is Jean back?"

"What the fuck are you talking about, Scott?" Anthony shouted through the door.

"Is Jean here?"

"No, I'm sorry, Darling. Jean ain't here. The newspapers say she's still gone. We heard a loud bang on the floor and came up here to see if ya were okay. We heard ya coughing. Ya were coughing a lot, Scotty. Are ya okay in there? Did ya fall down or something?" Barbara said.

"What time is it, please?" I asked.

"It's 8:10. I got my driver waiting outside for you. You want some breakfast before you go or not?" said Anthony.

"Just some water, please," I said.

"Okay, Darling. I'll get it for ya, Scotty."

I opened the door as Barbara ran down the long twisting oak staircase. Anthony was stood there with a handkerchief tied around his face. It made his eyebrows even more prominent than they already were. His eyes focused on my blood-stained vest.

"You look fuckin' awful, Scotty. You look like death warmed over."

"You look like a bandit," I smiled with pink teeth. He took a few steps back, away from me. He didn't smile back.

"I'm sorry, Scotty. But we've gotta look after our own health. I'm getting on in years now, I ain't a young man no more. I'm still recovering from this, ya know," he rubbed his stomach with his hands like an expectant mother.

"I know, Jessie James. It's okay. Don't worry yourself."

His face didn't change underneath the handkerchief and his eyes remained cold.

"I've tried to help you as much as I can, I'm sorry, Buddy, but it's time for you to ship out and go now. I don't give a fuck if it's the sanatorium or Palm Springs, but ya gotta go."

Barbara came back up the stairs with a glass of water. She had a white handkerchief tied around her face too and reached out the glass of water to me, as if to a rabid dog.

"It's Bonnie and Clyde," I said.

They didn't laugh. I took the glass from Barbara and closed the door. I drank the cold water and put on the same soiled, wilted clothes as the day before. I went to the basin under the window and ran cold water over my rough face and through my hair. It was cool and refreshing and I felt better.

I WALKED SHAKILY down the stairs to the front door like a man with a bad hangover, clinging to the banister and holding the newly soaked rag to my mouth. An overweight guy in his middle or late forties with a prominent nose that had been broken any number of times was stood smoking outside the front door. He nodded his large head at me and scratched at his red, week-old beard. He was wearing a black chauffeur's hat that didn't match the other clothes he was wearing. A green button-down shirt that wasn't tucked into his brown slacks and dirty tennis shoes.

"My names Rudy, I'm your driver for today. I'm takin' you to Palm Springs, Mr. Kelly."

His eyes flicked over my shoulder as he said it and I knew Anthony and Barbara were stood down the hall, observing with their bandit masks on. I turned around. They were there.

"I'm so sorry, Scotty. But come back when ya feeling better, okay? Ya know we always love to see ya," said Barbara.

Anthony was stood with his arm around her and nodded seriously at me.

"I hope you can talk to Jean, feel better about everything and go back to the hospital, Scotty." He nodded to the living room with a motion of his head and Barbara obediently walked that way out of sight, giving me a nervous little wave as she did.

Anthony came a little closer, a few steps. Wiped his hands on his shirt front and said, "I don't owe you nothin' now. As far as I'm concerned, we are both even now. You got no more favors coming from my end, Scotty. You understand that? You've cashed in all your chips with me and Mickey now. Whatever happens from now on in, I can't help you with, so don't embarrass us both by asking. Okay?"

"Sure, Tony," I stuck out my hand to shake, but he motioned me onto the front porch and closed the door with a disappointed shake of the head.

"Hell, that's a farshtunken way to say goodbye to a buddy. Especially, the macher Mr. Kelly," it was the driver, Rudy. I'd forgotten he was still standing there. We didn't shake hands either.

"You got any bags?" he asked.

I shook my head.

"Bubkes?"

"Yeah, bubkes."

"Okay then, let's go, Mr. Kelly."

I followed him down the garden pathway to the street and the black and wine-red automobile waiting there.

"Rolls Royce," I said.

"Yeah, this year's Rolls Royce Wraith. Mr. Cornero knows his automobiles, that's for sure."

"I've never been in a Rolls, before."

"Then today is a special day for you, Mr. Kelly. You're goin' to Palm Springs in style," he said tossing his cigarette butt into Barbara's flower patch.

He opened the door for me, I got in and settled down on the cool, black leather seats. Rudy got in the front, took off the cap, ran his fingers through his wavy, rust colored hair and put it on the seat beside him. Then he wrapped his arm around that seat and used it as leverage as he leaned around back to look at me.

"It's about three and a half hours give or take to Palm Springs, it's nearly nine now, so I reckon we'll get there about twelve thirty. You might as well take it easy and enjoy the ride. Alright, Mr. Kelly?"

"Yeah, Rudy. That's grand."

"You got the consumption, huh?"

"Do I look that bad?"

"Nah, you do look bad, but I know the look. My wife had the consumption a few years back, twenty-four-hour bed rest and all that. I'm sure you know well."

"How'd she get on?"

"It was rough for a while there. But she just gave birth to our sixth child a few months back. My eldest is fifteen. Grace. She's like her mother. Got her looks. She's smart too. She wants to go to college."

"Congratulations, Rudy. That's a big family. You should be proud."

"I am. Thanks, Mr. Kelly," he said.

He put the key in the ignition and the Wraith purred to life.

As Rudy pulled the Rolls out from the curb, I looked back towards Anthony's house. Anthony was stood out by the front door. He didn't wave. He stood there with his hands in his pockets. He was still wearing the handkerchief tied around his face. It was a strange sight. That pretty, white and baby blue house with the stocky hoodlum with a handkerchief hiding his face surrounded by all the flowers. I looked back until the image was lost from my view and then turned around again.

"Do you have any kids, Mr. Kelly?"

"Call me Scott."

"Alright, do you have any kids, Scott?"

"I've got a daughter. She's in New York with her mother."

He looked back at me in the rear-view mirror.

"I see. I used to be a New Yorker myself. Hell's Kitchen. You see her often? Your daughter?"

"Yeah, I see her often," I lied. It was easier than the truth.

"That's nice, then," he said, but he knew I had lied. The atmosphere's shift of weight in the Rolls was proof of that.

"I heard a lot about you, Boss. The Irish Marine. The Phantom. People say you were one of those shooters in on the Valentine's Day Massacre. Is that true?"

"How old do I look?" I cough-laughed.

He glanced in the rear-view mirror again.

"To be honest, I can't tell. What with the sickness, you know?"

"I'm only thirty. I was ten years old and still in Belfast, Ireland, waiting for a ship to bring us here, when that happened," I cough-laughed again.

"I feel kind of like a schlub now," he chuckled.

"Well, that's what happens when you listen to what people say. The people don't know shit, Rudy. Remember that."

"Talking about ages, I'm forty-one, as of next week."

"Happy Birthday for next week then," I said.

"Thanks, Boss. My wife, Maggie is gonna cook me a big dinner; steak, potatoes, gravy, the works."

"That's good, Rudy."

"Yeah, I'm looking forward to it."

I nodded and didn't say anything else, letting the conversation peter out. I felt very weak from the small talk, so turned instead and watched the landscapes decline from suburbs to open desert.

THE PHONE WAS ringing downstairs in the living room and woke me in a cold, clammy sweat from the dreams of the cliffs on Okinawa. I rolled over and put out my arm for Jean, but she was gone. I remembered she said she had an audition or something like that, a screen test, she'd told me excitedly. Her perfume and lipstick marks lingered on the waves of the white bed linen.

The telephone stopped ringing.

A sharp dullness was in between my eyes and an empty bottle of whisky was on the bedside table next to an overflowing ashtray. I leaned out of bed and picked up a pack of Luckies from the hardwood floor and looked inside. Empty. I picked a half-smoked cigarette with Jean's crimson lipstick marks on it from the ashtray and lit it. It tasted of Jean. I blew smoke at the ceiling.

The phone started ringing downstairs again.

I got up, went to the WC down the hall and took a piss, by the end of my stream the phone had stopped ringing again. I dropped the end of the cigarette down into the toilet bowl and flushed it away with the dark yellow piss. I washed my face with soap in the sink, trying to wash away thoughts of the beach house the day before, but I already knew it's the things you want to wash away most, that never wash out.

The telephone started ringing and then stopped.

She had been about my daughter's age.

The telephone downstairs started ringing again.

I went back into the master bedroom and I pulled on a pair of jockey shorts from the floor.

The telephone stopped ringing.

She had braids in her long blonde hair like my daughter.

I pulled on my slacks and a vest; the telephone started ringing again. My right eye ached.

I went down the stairs cursing, to answer it. The living room was a mess, with Jean's dresses slung over the furniture. Empty glasses, newspapers and another full ashtray were strewn across the coffee table. The telephone's ring pierced through my headache and I hurried to answer it to stop its incessant whine.

"Hello," I barked.

"Good morning, Mr. Kelly."

"Sure, good morning. What can I help you with?"

"I wanted to call and say thank you," the voice was very refined and rich. The voice of intelligence.

"Yeah? Thanks for what exactly?"

"Thank you for your service."

"Huh? it's early pal, and I've got things to do and a bad hangover. Get to the point, what are you selling and what are you taking about?"

"Thank you for your service in the war. I understand you were a Marine in the Pacific. You have my respect. War is a terrible, awful thing, and sometimes you have to go along with things you don't quite agree with. But you do go along because there isn't much else to be done. You have to go along, to get along. Sadly."

"Who is this?"

"I was a friend of a friend from New York. Thanks again for your service. Good day, Mr. Kelly."

He hung up and the line went dead. I put the receiver back on the hook and no sooner had I replaced it that it started ringing again. I picked it up and put it to my ear slowly.

"Who is this?"

"Scotty, it's me, Tony."

"Uh, it's you. What is it?"

"It's about yesterday. It's pretty fucked up, Scotty."

"Yeah, that fucking fat prick, Davy. The wife and daughter were in there. A woman and a fucking kid. He told me it was just the two marks."

"Davy's in a very bad way in the hospital, right now as we speak."

"He's lucky to be in a bad way. I was trying to kill the fat fuck."

"You left him there for the cops. That wasn't smart at all, Scotty. It's a good thing I sent a guy over there to check on things. He could get Davy out of there and to the hospital. You shouldn't have left Davy like that. It wasn't sensible at all."

"Sensible? He fucked up the job! He told me it was just the two men there. You better keep that fat snake far away from me, because if I see him again..."

"You've burnt a lot of bridges here, Scotty. Benny's angry as all hell about it."

"It was his fucking job. I did what he asked. I did more. I did a lot more."

"There's been talk of him putting out a job vacancy for you now."

"What the fuck? Why?"

"He had to pay a large chunk of cash to the cops, so they'd sniff around elsewhere. You see what I'm saying to you? A family killing? It's very bad for business, Scotty. And the word on the street is that all the dirty detectives that you had in your pocket have washed their hands of you, because of this shit."

"I'll talk to Benny and smooth all this shit out."

"I wouldn't advise that at all. He is under a lot of strain at the moment and ain't acting himself. You know all these court cases and fuckin' The Flamingo is hemorrhaging the money that Benny ain't skimming. New York is putting a lot of heat on him and he's buggier than his usual self. He's snuffed two guys himself this week, I heard. Piece of shit stole my ideas too."

"What do you advise I do then, Anthony? Because I ain't running. I ain't lambing it."

"That's what I called to talk about. I'm here with a friend of mine now, he has a proposition for you. I'll put him on, wait a moment."

I waited; the receiver was damp with sweat. A nasally voice came on the line.

"Hello, Scott Kelly, is it?"

"Yeah, who's this?"

"It's Mickey Cohen," Benjamin Siegel's number two man in Los Angeles. His underboss.

"Anthony said you've got a proposition for me."

"Wait a minute, I wanna say that I grew up with Davy. We knocked over a movie theater together when we were still in short pants, went to reform school together. A long fuckin' time I've known him. I'm disappointed that ya treat your colleagues with such disrespect. I'll discipline Davy myself if I think he needs disciplining. He ain't in trouble though, you're in trouble. You're in the worst kind of trouble with Benny. He's gonna put a job out on you. That's the word. What do ya think about that?"

"I'm not overjoyed about it, Mickey. But if that's the way it's gonna be, Benny had better send a fucking army's all I'm saying."

"You've got a lot of balls, Marine. A lot of chutzpah. That's good. Having balls will take you to the top of the world, but ya gotta have smarts too. Are ya smart, Scott?"

"Smarter than Benny and any goons he wants to try and send my way."

"It was a… what do ya call it? Rhetorical question. Me, I'm what you call a philanthropist and I'm gonna help ya get out of this farkakte situation, this pile of shit, you've found yourself swimming in."

"With the cops?"

"Don't worry about the cops. Benny already greased the right palms and they picked up some retarded shvartzer to take the rap for the beach house snuffs. He'll be sucking gas by Hanukkah."

"So how can you help me?"

"Beverly Hills, at his broad's house tomorrow night."

"What the fuck does that mean?"

"It's where Benny is going to be, tomorrow night."

"If you're saying, what I think you're saying, you're fucking crazy. I'll have the whole of New York City gunning for me. Every fucking soldier and associate from the five families."

"No, ya won't. It's kill or be killed and I'm guessing this isn't the only telephone chat, ya had this morning, am I right? Let's just say Benny has reached the end of the road and he's pissed on too many of his friend's shiny shoes to walk off into the sunset with that whore girlfriend of his. He's gotten too big for his breeches and thinks he's a fuckin' movie star. It's embarrassing. The meshuggener klumnik. People in high places have had enough. You understand what I'm saying to you, Scott Kelly, the Irish fuckin' Marine?"

I said I understood.

"I'll send someone over to your house with the finer details tonight. See ya around, Scott Kelly."

The previous telephone call made sense. Meyer Lansky in New York City. I hung up the telephone, went to the kitchen and poured myself a whisky. And then another.

I'D MET BENNY Siegel in early 1946 through Anthony Cornero and I met Anthony Cornero through a meathead called Mally. I'd barely got out of the service a few weeks before and Beth and I were struggling to make ends meet already. Our daughter was nearly six years old and all three of us slept in the same room in a one room apartment in a crime ridden place called Bunker Hill. I had thought that I'd get something good going after the service with the G.I bill, maybe go back to school. I was working as a clerk for the post office, until I could find something better. Trying to write about my experiences in Okinawa, but all the stories I'd mailed off, returned with rejection slips. I'd given up before I'd really even started.

I'd found adapting back into civilian life difficult to say the least. It didn't take too long to realize that I'd brought the war back with me. Beth and I started suffering from a suburban cabin fever. Bellowing hysterically at each other all day and night. Fighting and bickering, slamming doors and throwing things. Then our daughter had gotten really sick. Desperately ill with pneumonia. Call the priest kind of sick. The penicillin, the doctors and the medical care wiped out what little savings we had. My wife had to quit her temp job in an advertising agency in the city to care for our daughter around the clock. I stayed up all night, while my wife slept, holding our daughter in my arms, dabbing a damp cloth to her burning face and brow and talking to her softly, not sleeping myself at all, because I was scared the nightmares would come and I'd wake them both up screaming, killing ghosts, I'd already killed many times before in the war.

When we'd missed the weekly rent more than a few times and there wasn't much of a choice left, I'd gone down the street to a place I'd heard talked about in hushed tones around the pubs and bars of Bunker Hill: Mally's office. Mally's office wasn't really an office at all, it was just a butcher's shop that smelt heavily of blood and Mally was the butcher. Being a butcher wasn't his profession though, as he told me proudly, it was his hobby. His profession was loansharking and he lived for his work. He had a big goon with pock marks all over his face and cauliflower ears, who always stood by the cash register and didn't say anything. Mally gave loans to the poor of Bunker Hill with twenty percent vigorish a week. Which meant if you borrowed a hundred dollars, you'd have to pay back one hundred and twenty dollars. Or twenty dollars every week until you paid back the hundred bucks. Mally wasn't what I'd expected from a loan shark or a butcher. Short, squat, balding and he had a humpback. But what I had realized about him was, what he lacked in physical attributes he made up for in viciousness and malice. I had heard that if you didn't pay back what you owed, when you owed it by, Mally and the goon took you out back and sliced off the muscles from the backs of your legs. Which was unusual, because loan sharks usually didn't resort to heavy violence, it was bad for business. However, Bunker Hill being Bunker Hill, Mally was never too short of business. I had assessed him as being mentally unstable, dishonest, and dangerous as soon as I'd borrowed the damn money. Unfortunately for Mally, he didn't make the same assessments about me. That was his mistake, and, in this life, you have to pay for all your mistakes.

So, I'd borrowed a hundred bucks, paid for all of the rent and all of my daughter's medicine and medical expenses. She'd gotten better quickly. I'd worked a lot of extra hours as a clerk and Beth and I scraped together everything we had to pay back the loan a month later with its four weeks of vigorish. I'd gone down to the butcher's shop that day looking forward to getting the noose from around our necks and starting fresh again. Getting out of Bunker Hill with my family and going back to college on the G.I Bill, finally.

When I entered the Butcher's, Mally was tenderizing steaks on the butchery table with a cigarette hanging from the side of his mouth, squinting into the smoke. The goon stood like Frankenstein's monster next to him. When I'd put the cash on Mally's butchery table, he poked at it with a long bladed, bloody knife and said it wasn't enough. The vig went up to fifty percent because I didn't pay the vig the first week. He told me to get the rest of the cash before the end of the day or he and the goon would come to my apartment and take the debt out of my pretty wife and maybe even my daughter. The goon smiled and Mally squealed with laughter like a pig.

I left the shop, the bell ringing above my head and stood outside on the sidewalk. Staring into the traffic, kicking at the grit and dirt on the ground, sweating, raging, and thinking about what I would do.

Finally, I made up my mind and went back into the shop. The bell above the door rang again, Mally and the goon looked up and smirked. Mally went to say something, probably about it being quick, but before he could finish the sentence, I had picked up the steel meat tenderizer and swung it into the goon's face, chopping him through the cheeks, smashing teeth and shattering his jaw. He collapsed on the floor, flip-flopping like a fish, holding his mouth with bloody hands and screaming muffled screams. Mally went for the long knife on the table, but I brought down the meat tenderizer on his fat little hand. When he slumped to the floor next to the goon, holding his palm in agony, I had stood over him and took the meat tenderizer to his knees. First the left knee and then the right. The cracking noises were very satisfying. Mally shrieked. I asked him who he worked for and where I could find him. Then I took the cash out of my pocket, shoved it into his mouth and told him that all debts were paid up in full and not to fucking forget it. Kicked him in the balls, to drive my point home.

I went straight to the Italian restaurant where I would find Mally's boss, Anthony Cornero. I'd gone home first though, told Beth to take our daughter to the grocery store down the street until I came to get them later and grabbed my Colt 1911. When I'd gone to the restaurant, Anthony had asked me to sit down, listened to what I had to say, then offered me an espresso and a job in Salt Lake City, taking care of some big shot who had fucked the Italians over on a business deal. I'd accepted the espresso and the job. Salt Lake City had gone real bad, real quick but Tony had liked my style and kept offering me jobs. I kept accepting.

WHEN I AWOKE, Rudy was still driving. On a long quiet road surrounded by desert land. When he glanced into the rear-view mirror and saw I was awake, he spoke.

"You were talkin' in your sleep, you know?"

"Nothing too incriminating, I hope."

"My wife grinds her teeth. It drives me meshuga. Crazy. And we share a room with the youngest children. So, it's fair to say I don't get much shut eye."

"They're scared of the dark?"

"No, how do you mean?"

"The kids. They share the same room with you and your wife. They're scared of the dark?"

"Ah no, that's because we just got a two-room place at the moment. Me and my wife in one room with two of the youngest kids and the other four older kids share the other room. Money, it comes in one hand and out the other."

"I was there once. Like that. You should ask Anthony for a raise in salary. He's Italian, not a Jew. No offense intended."

"Ha, I can imagine his response already. Get the fuck outta here; he'd say."

"How about asking for some extra work, then? You see what I'm saying?"

"Ah, I did that. I mean, I started with Tony doin' the extra stuff. It started in his casino and then with breakin' up union strikes, moved on to collectin' what Anthony was owed, puttin' pressure on fellas, shit like that... Each time the money got a little better and a little better. After those jobs, I started doin' the more serious jobs..." he looked at me in the rear-view mirror again and rubbed the red stubble on his chin.

"You know the most serious jobs? You're California renowned for the most serious jobs. There was a time, I wanted to be like that. Be like you. Be a macher. Get myself set up with the cash, buy a nice house back in New York, buy nice things for my family, send my kids to a good school and then college. Be a renowned guy. But, after the first kind of serious job, I figured the money wasn't worth it, you know? The shit I had to do, it stayed with me long after the money was gone. So, I asked Tony for somethin' more... I don't know... I asked him for somethin' easier, because what I really wanted was somethin' that would cost me less... I'm sorry, that probably sounds foolish to you, huh?"

I held his eyes in the rear-view mirror for a long time and then said, "no, Rudy, it sounds like the most intelligent damn thing I've heard in a very long time."

I stared out of the window at the dusty landscape, bit into my bottom lip hard.

"Boss, would you mind if we stopped off somewhere to eat? I'm just about starved and maybe it'll do you good to eat somethin' too. It looks as though it's been a while since you last ate a proper meal. What do you say?"

"I could eat," I said

We stopped at about the halfway point before Palm Springs at the first roadside diner we came to.

THE ROADSIDE DINER was a long building that had cream and green paint flaking and peeling away from the wooden exterior. A fluorescent sign flashed red and read, 'Al's All-American Diner'. A smaller sign said, 'Home Made Pie'. Rudy had put his chauffeur cap back on his rusty head and led the way through the door. A bell rang above our heads and a waitress in her sixties with a kindly face and blue dyed hair showed us to a booth, told us the day;s specialties handing us some creased paper menus. The table was sticky, and someone had carved the word *SHIT* into the wooden surface. I wondered if it was an evaluation of the food.

"Why are all these places called 'Al's'? It's like everybody with the name Al suddenly realizes when they hit high school their only dream in life is to have a diner in the middle of nowhere," Rudy said.

"That's a good point. How about Rudy's Diner?"

"With my cookin'? People would pray after they eat, not before. I'd be more notorious than Murder Inc. What are you gonna have, Boss?"

"I'm gonna go for the apple pie and a black coffee. How about yourself, Rudy?"

"I'm gonna have the eggs and fries, I reckon. Expected you to order a steak or somethin' like that."

"Why?"

"I don't know. Maybe, because you're Scott Kelly, I didn't expect you to have the apple pie. It doesn't seem like somethin' a hard case would eat."

"I'm not a hard case, but I'm sure hard cases love homemade apple pie too."

"Are you sure you don't wanna order a steak or somethin'? It's not on the menu, but I'm sure they'll have somethin' out back."

"No, it's okay, I haven't eaten a slice of apple pie in years and I'm looking forward to it now. I don't have much of an appetite anyway. How long you been working for Anthony, Rudy?"

"Me and Tony, we go back a ways. First met him in '29, I was doin' laborin' work on his ship, you know, loadin', unloadin', donkey work mostly during the prohibition when everyone and their brother was getting rich except me. We were smugglin' rum from Mexico to California, some canary fuck sang, the government got tipped off and hijacked the ship just off the coast. We all took a pinch, Tony included. While bein' transported by the rail to prison, we beat down the guards and jumped off the train. I broke my leg in the fall and the cops found me in a wooden shack not far from where we'd jumped. Tony got free and clear, though. I got five years in San Quentin. When I finally got out of that hellhole, Tony remembered me and helped me out. Gave me a job workin' security in his place 'The Meadows' just outside of Vegas, you know the place?"

"Sure, I know it. That place was the reason I quit gambling."

"Well, I worked there for a couple of years and then Tony started askin' for help with other jobs and I worked my way up, then worked my way back down and here I am," he waved his hands in front of his chest like he'd just finished a magic trick.

"Well, that sounds like a hard case to me, Rudy."

"Maybe I'll have a slice of that apple pie, too then."

"Apple pie, the breakfast of champs. When did you start driving him around?"

"Just after he got shot. I was the one who was drivin' him to and from the hospital for his checkups."

"The Milk Carton Assassination Attempt, I like to call it."

"What do you mean? Milk carton?"

"I'll tell you that story after you've eaten."

"I'm curious now. I hadn't heard nothin' about no milk cartons. Tell me later before we get to Palm Springs, if it's a long story. Nothin' is better on a long drive than a long story. Anyhow, how about you? When did you first start workin' for Tony?

"February 1946, I think. Just after I got out from the Marines."

"What was it like? The war, I mean?"

"Hell. The smells, the sounds, the taste of the place."

"Did you kill a lot of the Japanese?"

"If one isn't too many, a thousand isn't enough."

"I can't imagine what that would be like. I never did that kind of job before."

"I thought you said you did serious jobs for Anthony?"

"Yeah, but not the most serious kind, you know what I mean," he made a pistol with his hand and pointed it at the napkin holder.

"It's not that much different from the other serious work. Hurting someone bad, so they can't work anymore, their family suffers too and putting an end to someone. It's basically the same thing, following orders, like in the war."

"How'd you mean?"

"Soldiers get told to go somewhere and take something or go somewhere and hurt someone or make someone dead. Soldiers are all just hard cases, killing for another hard case who's on a level above them. It's all the same bullshit. Except in Los Angeles, you get paid a helluva lot more. The military gave me the best kind of training to make the best kind of money doing all the worst kind of things." It was my turn to make a pistol shape with my hand.

"I think you've got to have somethin' special to be like that."

"Special?" I laughed out loud. Heaved. Hacked into my hands. "No, not something special, more like something broken." I tapped at my head.

"I should probably mention to you that I was the one who picked Davy up that day," Rudy said.

"How's that?" I asked

"At the beach that day, the beach house, I was the one who picked Davy up and took him to the hospital."

"You should have left him there. Would've saved me a lot of trouble and we wouldn't have been driving to Palm Springs today."

He nodded and shuffled the menus on the table. The waitress came over and took our orders. Rudy sat looking out the windows at the occasional passing automobile and I held the cloth to my face until the food came. When it did, we ate in silence, slowly. Poking at our food with our forks and trying to think of conversation but failing and after when it was time to get moving again, I paid from my last cash roll and left a good tip for the old waitress. I felt a little better for having eaten and the hot coffee was good. I felt a little more positive, but when we walked back out to the Rolls, I hacked and retched until I vomited onto the gravel and Rudy had to help me back to the car.

CHAPTER 8

WE HAD A good table by the stage. The Nat King Cole Trio were playing that night. Jean sat with her elbows on the white tablecloth, her chin rested on her entwined fingers, gazing at me with those big blue eyes. She wore her long chestnut colored hair down and a tight, black cocktail dress at my request. It was her twenty-fourth birthday and I'd brought her to the Chi-Chi Club in Palm Springs to celebrate. I glanced up from the menu to see her looking at me. She blew a kiss, winked, and giggled. I shifted my chair closer to her, kissed her lips softly, tasting champagne and her lipstick on my tongue, feeling the side of her face in my palm. She pulled her mouth away from mine.

"You're making me all hot and flustered, Scotty and we only just got here."

"You're just so beautiful, I can't help myself," I pulled her face roughly towards mine and kissed her again. Her tongue slid over mine, flickering. I ran my hand up her smooth leg under the table, hidden by the white tablecloth, feeling her open up for me just a little, teasing me and teasing herself. She bit my lip and opened her thighs a little wider so I could feel the warm moisture on her silken panties. I could hear the grumbling comments people were making at other tables, but I didn't care.

"Oh Scott, don't. Don't. You're making me half-crazy and we're in public."

"If you're half-crazy, then I'm at full-crazy right now. How about ditching this joint and going back to the hotel for room service and dessert," I winked.

She sipped her champagne and grinned into the glass.

"You're like a teenage boy, but that's why I love you."

We kissed again, softer this time, glanced around at the other tables and the disapproving faces, falling into fits of giggles.

"I should have gotten us a table at the back, in a corner. What was I thinking getting the table nearest the stage?" I laughed when I said it, but it had only really been half a joke. Jean made me want her all the time. Everywhere. I had lost track of the strange and unusual places we had made love. In a park, at a racetrack, in a casino bathroom, under a bridge, an alleyway, in my bar on the bar, a playground, a train carriage and a tennis court, to have named a few. I guessed we really were like a couple of teenagers.

"It'll be more exciting if we wait until later tonight at the hotel, and anyway I'm famished, Darling. Let's order some food before the band starts," said Jean.

I clicked my fingers in the air, faux pompous, a waiter rushed over and took our order; I ordered the baby lobster in a half shell and the Eastern Prime New York cut steak and Jean ordered the French-fried jumbo shrimps and the Filet Mignon. I told the waiter to send over another bottle of champagne.

"Scotty, this is the best birthday, I've ever had. Thank you so much. You're so sweet."

"Well, it's not over yet. I've got a little surprise for you later too."

She put her hands to her cheeks in mock surprise and smiled teasingly.

"Really? Something in the hotel? Is that what you're calling it now?"

"Yeah, that as well, but something here."

THE FOOD WAS good, and I was just content to watch Jean eat a lot and drink underneath the bright lights of the stage. The spotlights making her look even more stunning than she already was. She really was a babe made for Hollywood and I was sure there were a lot of envious men in the room wondering exactly how a guy with a face like mine got a woman with a face like hers. Often, I wondered that myself.

When Jean finished eating, she dabbed the sides of her lips with a napkin. It made me smirk, because she had always done the same thing after she had taken me in her mouth the French way.

"What are you smirking about, Mister?" she slapped my arm playfully.

"Nothing, nothing. I'm just happy is all."

She sipped her champagne and watched me with her blue, blue eyes as she swallowed. Then she thought for a few seconds and said,

"Really?"

"Really, What?"

"Are you happy here with me?"

"Yeah, of course I am. I wouldn't be happier with anybody else here with me, but you. You must know that by now. I'm crazy about you, Jean."

"You never say 'I love you' when I say it."

I quoted a Yeats poem about a blanket and she stuck her tongue out in mock disgust.

"You're such a romantic. Now I know why you have all those poetry books at your place, so you can quote dead poets instead of saying what you should really say. What I'm *waiting* to hear."

"This is the only poetry I need," and under the table again, I ran my hand up her thigh and teased her there. Our mouths found each other's and she sighed, the deep kind of sigh a woman releases to let you know that she's yours for the taking. She's ready.

The emcee came up onto the stage and joshed with the audience, cracking jokes, before he announced the main act, and everyone applauded and whistled.

Nat King Cole came out, waved to the crowd, smiled, bowed, sat down at the piano and adjusted his microphone a little before speaking into it.

"Good evening Ladies and Gentlemen, my name's Nat King Cole and this is the Nat King Cole Trio."

113

Two other spooks came out from behind curtains at opposite sides of the stage and stood next to large stringed instruments. The crowd clapped and cheered. I looked at Jean, her eyes were sparkling, and she looked like an excited little girl. I could see the way she had looked when she was a child as she gazed up at the stage, awestruck and fascinated. Nat waved the crowd down to hush them and then continued, "The first song we are going to perform tonight is one of my favorites and I hope it's a favorite of yours too, it's a little ditty called, 'I love you, for sentimental reasons'."

The crowd cheered and clapped again. Jean clapped and whistled in the direction of the stage with her fingers in her lips. I retrieved the long box from out of my sport coat pocket, clicked it open and slid it over the tablecloth to her. She looked down and gasped with her hands to her face. She stayed like that for over a minute, frozen and then she took the diamond necklace out and held it in her fingers gently, gazing at it with teary eyes.

I whispered in her ear, "That's not all. Listen," I waved to the man behind the piano. He looked over at us and smiled, saluted me and said, "this song is for Miss Jean Spangler, it's her twenty-fourth birthday today and my good pal Scott wants her to know... I love you for sentimental reasons..." he sang.

Jean was crying. I'd seen her cry a few times, but I'd never seen her cry with this much happiness before. Breathless. She adjusted her chair, turned her back to me and lifted up her hair and I kissed the back of her neck, the bumps of her spine, and clasped the diamond necklace around her neck. Tears were still sliding down her face and she kept waving her hand at the tears to try and stop the flow, the way women do. I pushed my chair back, stood up and held out my hand to her. The audience cheered. By that point, too drunk and too happy to give a damn what anybody thought.

"Dance with me Jean."

"What? No, are you crazy, Scotty? I'll die of embarrassment. I'll just die."

I kept my hand out. Someone in the crowd whistled loudly

and a woman shouted out for Jean to get up.

"Dance with me Jean. Everyone in this place is watching us, so you can't say no now," I chuckled, shrugged to the crowd. Playing it up.

She took my hand, stood up gracefully and laced her arms around my neck. I ran my hands around her hips, rested them on the small of her back and we danced like that, by our table, holding each other's gaze the entire time. It was almost like making love with our eyes. She let tears fall onto my shoulder and kissed my neck softly. After a while, a number of other couples stood up to dance and by the time Nat had finished the song, we had every couple in the place dancing slowly around us.

THAT NIGHT IN the hotel she'd worn only the necklace as we'd made love on the carpet. Jean on top of me, slowly easing herself up and down. The necklace bouncing in rhythm with her swollen, pert breasts, occasionally slowly coming to a stop, drinking champagne from a glass on the floor next to us and passing me drops of it with her mouth. Easing herself up and down faster and faster until I couldn't hold it any longer. She lifted up and off and finished me with her mouth. After she sipped champagne smiling at me all the while whispering, "This was a perfect birthday for me, Scotty. I love you."

Afterwards, we showered together slowly and sat on the balcony in our hotel robes, drinking champagne lazily. Looking at the dark silhouettes of the San Jacinto Mountains. I had never felt as content as I did at that moment. I hadn't had relapses or replays or any bad dreams for weeks. I drank my champagne slowly and thought that everything was going to go well for me.

"Oh no, I forgot!" she said, putting her glass down and going back into the bedroom.

When she came back, she held a small, brown paper bag and passed it to me.

"What's this?" I asked.

"I know it's not your birthday until December, but I wanted to give it to you while we were here together in Palm Springs. So, when you use it, you'll always remember me and this special place," she waved her hands toward the flowers climbing up the balcony around us, at the palm trees below and then to all the city lights and mountains in the distance.

I took a small box out of the paper bag, untied a small ribbon, and opened it. It was a Zippo cigarette lighter with my name inscribed on it in cursive 'Scott'.

"Look at the other side," she said placing her hands on my leg and leaning into me.

I took the zippo out of the box and turned it over in my palm. *'From the one, who loves you most,'* inscribed on it.

"Ah, wow. I don't know what to say. I've never gotten something like this before from anyone, Jean. Thank you very much. I really appreciate this so much," I said, flicking the lighter and starting a flame. In the light from the zippo, I could see she was crying again. I kissed her face and tasted her tears, pulled her on top of me and we made love again in silence on the balcony, surrounded by the smell of flowers, the chirping of crickets and the silhouettes of the mountains on the horizon beyond us.

We stayed in bed the entirety of the next day and left the following night, making promises to return to Palm Springs together.

We never got the chance, so we never did.

"PENNY FOR YOUR thoughts, Boss?"

I startled, surprised by being torn away from the memories. Some of the few good memories I had left that weren't contaminated shit.

"What?" I mumbled.

"Sorry, Boss, just, you know you've been lookin' out of the window for the last couple of hours and I wondered what you were thinkin' about?"

"I was thinking about the past."

"Good memories, huh?"

"Some of the best. I was thinking about Palm Springs a couple of years back."

"Ah, Palm Springs, I getcha'. Well, we're almost there now. Look."

I leaned forward, looked through the windshield and could see the city in the distance. Then, I could feel more coughs boiling in my chest and working their way up my throat. I wound down my window and started to breath the dry desert air hoping to stifle the episode, but it came anyway. The heaviest load of blood so far. I coughed into the rag and collapsed sideways onto the seat, fighting for breath. My lungs filling with blood, slowly drowning me in a Rolls Royce on the road to Palm Springs. My right eye ached. Rudy swerved, pulled over to the side of the road, got out and opened the back door, helping me out. I sank down heavily on the gritty, dusty ground, spraying the dirt with splashes of my blood. When I pulled myself back together and looked at the mountains, I thought about everything that had changed in my life since the last time I'd seen them. Jean was gone and I was probably dying. But the mountains hadn't changed at all, they had remained the same and I wished that Jean and I could have stayed on that balcony that night and like the mountains never changed.

Rudy sat down beside me and looked over at the same hills. He reached into his hip pocket and brought out a silver flask and passed it to me. Shaking it as he did.

"It's gin. It might do you some good, Boss."

I took the flask, "Thanks," I uncapped it, raised it in the air. "Sláinte," I said.

"L'chaim," Rudy said.

We both sat there in the dirt and the afternoon sun, staring out at the desert, the brown shrubs, and the mountains in the distance. After a while Rudy said, "I hope whatever it is you're goin' to Palm Springs for is worth it, Boss, because lookin' at you right now, I think that anything other than your last rights, might just be a bridge too far."

I took another hit from the flask and drained it.

"I'm trying to get back something that was taken from me."

"Is it worth dyin' for?"

"It isn't worth living without," I said and passed him back the empty flask.

I reached into my pocket and handed Rudy the folded piece of lined legal paper and he unfolded it and nodded to himself like he was agreeing with it.

"Room 7B. Desert Inn. Palm Springs. That won't be hard to find at all, Boss. It's probably the oldest and most well-known place to stay in the whole of Palm Springs."

"I just hope the people who are staying there aren't hard to find," I said.

"Davy?"

"No, the girl that is with him."

"Tony told me a little about it."

"Did he?"

"Yeah, but he told me just to get you there and leave you. Drive straight back to the city. I think he is worried about somethin' goin' bad in Palm Springs."

"That's pretty sound advice, Rudy and Tony's probably right. He usually is."

We sat like that for another ten minutes or so until my wheezing had eased off and I had control of my functions again. And then finally Rudy stood up, brushed the dust off his slacks, helped me up to my feet and we walked stumbling back to the automobile again. I stopped once more to look back at the mountains before I got into the Rolls and we pulled out once more onto the road to Palm Springs.

CHAPTER 9

THE CITY OF Palm Springs rose out of the desert to greet us like a mouth swallowing us up into its sun-bleached motel lined streets. Flowers, flashy signs on gaudy bars, palm trees and eateries flashed past the automobile like voices from the past. I'd only really seen the place in the darkness before, only after sunset when the neon lights cast a red and blue haze over the city and the sounds of jazz and parties seeped out of the buildings intermingling with the noises of the streets. During the afternoon Palm Springs seemed an entirely nocturnal animal to me, slumbering until the night came to resurrect it.

A frontier town that had been stolen from the natives and grown quickly into a playground for the rich and famous. A place with a haunting kind of beauty, like the unspoiled parts of Okinawa that hadn't been touched by the war, little reservoirs of nature or civilization. Why had Jean decided to return to Palm Springs without me? I couldn't understand it. We'd always said we'd go back together. We'd pledged it to each other on the balcony that night.

Rudy drove past the Chi-Chi Club. It was closed. It looked dead and derelict in the early afternoon daylight.

I'd decided before even leaving Anthony's office the previous night that I was going to kill Davy just as soon as I could get Jean away from him. If Mickey wanted a war, he could have one, but there was no chance in hell of Davy Ogul leaving Palm Springs alive.

Rudy swung the Rolls Royce through black iron gates that screamed 'THE DESERT INN' across them in gold. Parked the Rolls in a shady spot underneath a cluster of palm trees close to the main entrance.

"I won't be staying here, but go and get me a room, please

Rudy," I said and peeled off a few more bills from the last declining cash roll.

"Sure, Boss. Don't go anywhere, huh?"

"I won't," I grunted. Too drained to grin. I waited in the automobile wheezing into the rag and he came back soon after shaking a key with a large copper colored fob on it.

"I got you a room that overlooks the pool terrace at the side and rear of the hotel. You're on the second floor, a few doors down from the one you're lookin' for. Davy's room. Here's the change."

He handed over the key and a few bills. I took the key but left the cash in his hand.

"That's a tip for your driving skills, Rudy."

"Thanks, Boss. But there's about fifty dollars left here."

"It's a small tip, Rudy and here's another; you should get back to Los Angeles now. I'll be alright on my own from here on out."

"Are you sure, Boss? Let me help you to your room at least."

"I said I'll be fine. You know what Anthony said. You've played your part out. Palm Springs is about to do the jitterbug and your job was to get me to my final destination. You've done that now. Go back to Los Angeles, Rudy and get yourself out of this life."

I swung myself out of the Rolls and readjusted the pistol into the small of my back, sliding off the safety. Rolled my shoulders back, did up my sport coat buttons and banged on the top of the driver's side roof.

"See you around, hard case."

"Yeah, I'll be seein' you, Boss." He made a grim smile with his mouth and tightened his fists on the steering wheel. As I walked in the sun, I could still feel him watching me as I made my way around the hotel to the pool side terrace where blood-red flowers were blossomed all over the white walls, the sweet smell of nectar on the air.

The desert heat scorching and heavy. The hotel humming. Groups of people seated at tables eating lunch and drinking excitedly or lounging individually on sun chairs reading newspapers. I tried to stroll casually around the clusters of people and tables, staying in the shade of the walls. Quickly checking the faces around me. Then I saw him. My heart started drumming crazily in my chest. On the other side of the pool. Davy. Finding him had been much easier than I'd expected. But, then again, he thought he was untouchable, so had no reason to hide. Sitting underneath a large striped parasol. He had his whalelike back to me, wearing a maroon shirt stained dark with sweat under the armpits and down the back. I could recognize that fat, bald head anywhere. The crown of his skull now crisscrossed with pink, fleshy scars and I felt a dull kind of satisfaction. My heart still hammered my chest. Jean. Jean. Jean. She had to be close by. I could smell her perfume on the breeze.

I stopped by the pool, acting like I was admiring the blue water and the girls in bikinis, as I estimated the situation. Keeping my body loose and relaxed. My eyes rolled around in my skull, searching frantically for Jean. She wasn't at the table, nor in the pool, nor at the bar. She wasn't anywhere else that I could tell. I couldn't see her face anywhere. She must have been in the hotel room. I could feel her there on the hot afternoon air.

I weighed up the situation again, squinting over at Davy's location. He was smoking a cigar and waving it around as he talked animatedly to two men. Not Jean as I'd counted on, but two men. One an athletic looking guy in his middle thirties, wearing a brown suit and the other guy younger looking, pink faced, heavier set and wearing the dark blue uniform of the LAPD. He wasn't wearing his cap. Off duty and way out of the jurisdiction of the LAPD. The silver and gold badge on his chest glistened in the sun. Two of LAPD's finest. So, two of Davy's crooked cop associates were with him now, but what were they doing in Palm Springs and where was the third cop? No one else around the pool even remotely resembled a police officer. Still pretending to be checking out the pool, I looked back over. Evaluating.

The officer in blue was laughing a lot, the annoying kind of fake guffawing and slapping his knee like Davy was a laugh a minute. He had a service revolver in a holster on his hip and a nightstick in his belt. The other guy in the brown suit, still wearing his jacket to conceal his shoulder holster was clean shaven, somber faced and had his mousy hair oiled back on his head in a shabby pompadour. He'd drink from his coffee cup, nod, and then study the perimeter of the pool, an LAPD detective, I guessed. Our eyes momentarily snagged, I quickly turned away from the pool, taking the key fob out of my slacks' pocket, putting on an act, a tipsy tourist who'd forgotten his room number.

I hurried up some stone steps leading to the second-floor terrace area. Took a chance, glanced over again. Shit! The detective in the brown suit was still watching me, pinching a cigarette to his lips and frowning, while Davy continued to talk animatedly and the cop in blue continued to laugh it up, slapping his knee. Then I felt it, the storm in my lungs brewing once again, rolling like thunder in my air sacs. Shit! I cursed myself under my breath again, counting down blue doors and gold door numbers until I found the blue door with the number on it that matched the number on the copper fob in my clammy, trembling hand. Still putting on the drunken tourist act, I quickly got the key into the hole, pulled the door open and stepped into the calm of the room, shutting the door behind me. Leaning back against it, the storm hit, I let it go and broke into a heavy fit of coughs. Went for my rag, but my pocket was empty. I'd left it in the back of the Rolls. The hemorrhage seeped through my fingers. I let the blood grow fat and drip to the floor like a hard rain.

RAINDROPS GREW FAT on the rim of my helmet and fell. It was always raining here. Always raining on the road to Shuri Castle. Always raining in this darkened theater, soaking the seats and the screen.

Shuri castle. The Japs' last stronghold on the island of Okinawa. The hard, relentless rain washed everything into a shit-colored brown. The mud seeped into my flesh. I felt it there festering beneath my skin. In hell there were no fires and no brimstone. Hell was a shit-stained landscape of mud, broken, naked trees, craters overflowing with wretched rainwater, smoking tanks, the screams of mortar shells colliding with the earth and the dead. Always the dead. Always the dead and always the maggots. They wriggled and danced over the faces of the corpses scattered everywhere, dodging raindrops. Feasting and growing grotesque. The faces of the dead always grinned at me here, knowing more than I. The stench of the island crawled into my mouth, infested my nostrils and when I ate, I tasted the mud, the rot, the death and I vomited bile, unable to eat because everything tasted of the stench.

The mud sucked at my boots and I quick marched along a road of good intentions to a dishonorable end. They told the leftovers of us, the few remaining Marines, to take Shuri castle. If we took Shuri castle, the Japs would be finished with and it would be over. The Japs would quit and surrender. Shuri castle, the last stop before home. Shuri castle the heart at the center of the beast. But the dead grinned, knowing that I would never really leave the island. I had always been there, and I'd never leave. I was always the dead.

BACK AT THE one room apartment in Bunker Hill, California, smoking a cigarette by the window. Fighting sleep instead of a war. My daughter cried out into sheets of black; she feared the dark.

THE MUD WAS up to my knees. I found a small boy, naked and shivering, cowered behind the wreck of a destroyed half-track, covered in muck and insects. I got down next to him on my knees and held my water flask to his mouth. I tried to wipe his eyes clear of dirt. He was quiet and he trembled there in the mud.

I TOOK HER in my arms and wiped the tears from her eyes, they were a very deep grey and I saw the same eyes in the mornings staring back at me the mirror when I shaved my tired face.

I SAW A woman's legs and ass sticking out from underneath the half-track. She was naked too. Her skin porcelain white and dried blood caked around her inner thighs; bamboo sticks had been shoved deeply into her pussy and asshole. I saw maggots writhing there.

SHE WANTED ME to tell her a story about a castle and a knight in shining armor. A story with a happy ending. She was sick with pneumonia. Burning up with fever.

SNIPER FIRE KNOCKED Marines down into the mud and they just didn't get up again, like drunks tripping over and kicking out, then lying still to sleep it all off. Sleep it off buddy and you'll feel better tomorrow. Machine gun fire roared and mortar fire ripped up the earth. My right eye ached. A Marine to my left disappeared into a lumpy red mist. Losing my humanity in an inhuman place at an inhuman time. Unsure of who I was or who I'd been. I saw the castle in front of us. Once a marvel to the eye, but now just a ruined shape of things.

HER LONG, BLONDE hair hung in braids, her bangs stuck to her forehead in moist clumps and she shivered and looked into my face.

SNIPER FIRE AND machine gun rounds struck brown boulders, shells of burnt-out houses. We ducked our heads down, crawling in the mud and shit. And then finally the rain stopped. The sounds of mortar fire and artillery ceased. The sniper bullets began to miss and then drizzled off with the rain. Machine gun fire hushed and faded away. Everything stopped. I thought I could hear the Pacific Ocean and then we saw the red, white, and blue raised above the castle ruins and we cheered, fixed bayonets and ran screaming into the broken walls of the castle.

I HELD A damp cloth to her forehead and her small fingers held my hand tightly in the dim candlelight.

WE DRAGGED THE remaining Japs cringing out of their holes and machine gun nests into the mud and bashed their heads in with rifle butts, ran them through with bayonets and shot them slowly, almost savoring the kills. I'd murdered them so many times that it had become the same as taking a shit. We found Jap soldiers and civilians crouched, huddled together in small caves below the castle. I sent in the soldiers with the flamethrowers strapped on their backs to light them all up. Watched them all burn.

I STRUCK A match and lighted another candle on the bedside table. The flame sparkled on her damp skin and glistened in her grey eyes so damn brightly.

BEFORE THE SMOKE had cleared, while it was still dark and billowing out from the holes, we blew up the entrances with our grenades. An old man with long, straggly grey hair in raggedy pants, hobbled over to me screaming with moist eyes, waving his hands like a crow, gesturing towards the buried caves and screaming at me in a language I couldn't understand and didn't want to understand. I laughed because I couldn't cry.

I hated because I couldn't love. He slapped at me with feeble hands that were wet with the rain. He slapped at my face. I slid the blade of my bayonet smoothly up under his ribs. There was nothing else I could do. I felt the blade hit bone, collapsed a lung. His eyes were very dark, wet and warm. He was very surprised. His eyes widened and became very white against his tanned skin. He continued to shout at me and point to the cave. I pulled the bayonet out of his ribs and pushed it slowly into his chest, we fell into the muck together. I pushed the bayonet deeper through the bone into the heart of the beast. His naked feet kicked and slid in the brown sludge and made shapes of ruined things. After everything he seemed so unconvinced and utterly confused. I left him there in the mud to die.

I HELD HER tight in my arms, wiped her cheeks with my fingers, rocked her slowly, kissing her forehead until she yawned, closing her eyes.

IT HAD STARTED to rain again, I watched raindrops grow fat on the rim of my helmet.

THERE WAS NOTHING else I could do. Everything had been taken. I told her I was sorry, but I didn't have any stories with happy endings, this wasn't a story with a happy ending, because there were none. I told her to close her eyes again and sleep. Just sleep and you'll feel better when you awake.

I OPENED MY eyes and found myself lying prone. My face on the fuzzy, blue carpet, stained brown with droplets of my disease. I got up slowly and staggered to the window, dizzy with vertigo, moving the curtain slightly at the edge nearest the wall. Gently making a gap there, I peered out over the pool. A sniper's nest. Davy and the cops were still there. The detective in brown was talking now and Davy and the cop in blue were listening intently, nodding along. The detective in brown talked with his hands a lot and pointed down at the table a few times as if to hit home a point. I felt trickles of blood move down through the scraggly beard that had grown on my face the last few days and wiped my mouth with the sleeve of my sport coat. I had the impression they were talking about the heroin Davy had made off with and that they were holding for him. They continued to talk, and I continued to watch.

Ten minutes went by, then the cop in blue looked at his wristwatch, drained his beer and said something to the detective in brown. Both the cops started a brief conversation, ignoring Davy who picked up his glass and shook it impatiently at the waiter stood by the bar, who rushed over and gave him a refill from a bottle of rum. The cops stood up, took turns shaking hands with Davy and then strolled around the pool, towards the main entrance and out of sight. The cop in brown wiped his hand on his jacket sleeve as he walked away.

Fifteen more minutes passed. Davy had drunk three more glasses of rum, said something to the waiter and threw down some cash on the table. He waited for the loose change, stood up and started his slow, heavy waddle around the pool without leaving a tip. His bald head glaring in the sun. I knew he had to return to his room by passing by my door. I waited; the pistol gripped in my hand. He disappeared out of sight and I waited by the window for his silhouette to darken the curtains. Heard him wheezing from the effort of the stairs through the glass. Waited fifteen seconds and then went to the front door, opened it as quietly as I could and slid out several feet behind the fat fuck. My heart started beating faster, Jean's face in my mind. I'd finally see her again. Take her away with me and everything would be all right. I gained on Davy as he took his room key out of his slacks pocket and jiggled it in his fingers, whistling to himself. I got up real close and stuck the Colt in his flabby back.

"Don't make a scene you fat fuck. Just keep walking."

He gasped like an old woman and then tried to regain his

composure.

"Soldier Boy?! Ya look like shit. How ya been?" he slurred.

"Shut your fat, fucking mouth and go to your door. Open it slowly."

"They sent you?" he shrugged, faking impartialness. Faking bravado.

"Open the door slowly and keep your hands where I can see them, or you'll get a bullet in the back."

He opened the door and stepped in slowly, hesitating and I pushed him as hard as I could further into the room, kicking the door shut behind me. He turned around to face me, mock disappointment on his face.

"I'm disappointed they sent a fuckin' degenerate child killer like you to punch my ticket."

"Shut the fuck up and keep your hands in the air. Jean!? Jean!?" I walked into the main area of the room. Keeping my pistol trained on his chest the whole time. The room had the exact same layout as mine. One king sized bed, a writing desk, light blue carpeting, a small bar, a chair, a small sofa. I couldn't see her. She wasn't there.

"Jean!? Jean!?" I opened the bathroom and looked inside. Just white porcelain. Empty.

"Who the fuck ya lookin' for Soldier Boy?" he slurred again. Still stood in the middle of the room, next to the bed with his hands up, beads of sweat all over his face like teenager acne. I went over and stuck the pistol in his gut, frisked him to make sure he had nothing on him.

"Where the fuck is Jean?"

"What? I don't know where that stupid little whore is."

I chopped him in the throat with the side of my open hand and then brought the pistol butt down heavy on the bridge of his nose. Blood burst out, sprayed over his face and maroon shirt. I was happy that I'd finally seen someone else's blood flow instead of my own. Davy fell down to his knees holding his face. Blood seeped through his fingers. I put the pistol to his head.

"I've been waiting a long time to put a bullet in your head,

Davy. Now, where's Jean? Is she here at the hotel? Somewhere else in Palm Springs? Tell me, now!" I clicked back the hammer on the pistol and pressed it harder into his greasy forehead.

"Wait! Wait! Mickey sent ya, right? Cos' he found out about the brown, right?"

"Yeah, he fucking knows you stole the junk."

"He found out the cops sold it? I didn't know shit about that. They got a contact in New York. They sold the H without me knowin' bout it. But I got the money here, see…" He went to reach under the bed. I kicked him hard in the mouth. He screamed and rolled over onto his back, flopping around like a beached whale. A couple of yellowed teeth rolled onto the carpet like dice. I reached under the bed and pulled out a heavy, black leather briefcase and a shotgun. I put the shotgun on the sofa behind me and put the briefcase on the bed.

"Open it. Open it," he moaned. He pointed his bloody fingers at the case.

I pointed the pistol at him as I fumbled with the clasps on the case and it swung open to show bundles of cash and a lot of them.

"See, I told ya. Take it back to Mickey. I'll go to Mexico. He'll never see me again. I'll never be a problem for him again. That cash'll buy me out. Okay? It's okay."

He sat up and pulled his shirt out of his slacks and used it to wipe his nose and face. I sat down on the sofa and pointed the pistol at him again.

"Put your hands on your head. Lock your fingers together."

"Take the money bac—"

"Shut the fuck up, you fat prick. I'm not here for the heroin or the cash or whatever the fuck you're thinking. I'm here for Jean. Where is she?"

"Jean? I don't know. She ain't with me."

"I asked where the fuck is she?"

"I said, I don't know. She was just a whore I fucked for a little while. That's all. I don't know nothin' about her, don't care neither. Why ya lookin' for her? Ya her pimp or something?"

I started coughing, let the blood fly out of my mouth like spittle, the pistol shaking in my hand.

"Ya pretty sick, huh? What do the slant eyes call that? Karma, Soldier Boy? It's Karma, ain't it?" he gap-toothed smirked.

"Jean was here with you and now she's missing. Anthony told me she was here in Palm Springs with you. I want to know where she is."

"So what? Ya wanna know and people in hell want ice water. She came here all the time with a bunch of the other fellas. Not just me. Go ask around."

"What do you mean?"

He snickered, "I mean she was a little whore that got passed around a lot. A LOT. She changed hands more times than a crumpled dollar bill, I tell ya. It was just my turn with her, that's all. No mystery in it."

I stood up and walked over to him, Davy cowered with his hands in the air, covering his face. I kicked him hard in the ribs, heard something crack and he screamed low and hoarse. He rolled over holding his flabby side and snarled at me.

"Even ya best buddy Tony was fucking that little cooze. Didn't know that, did ya? We all fucked that broad. Girl was a degenerate whore. Nice titties though. Nice tight little pussy." He stuck his tongue out and wiggled and wagged it around the room, making slurping sounds.

I took a pillow from the bed, placed it on his thick calf, put the pistol's business end to the pillow and shot him. The sound came out like a dull thud and feathers twisted through the air like snowflakes on Christmas Day. I got the pillow shoved tight over his face as he bucked and screamed. I went over to the window and briefly looked out over at the pool. None of the revelers seemed to have noticed. All the physical effort was making my breathing strangled. Panting and heaving again. Running out of time. The heaving would lead to coughing, coughing would lead to hemorrhaging and finally I'd pass out and Davy and the cops would bury me alive somewhere out in the desert in an unmarked grave. I stumbled back over to Davy. He was crying and mumbling to himself. I sat down on the bed and put my shoe on his chest holding him down.

"I want to know exactly when was the last time you saw Jean? I'll give you sixty seconds to spill what you know, if you wanna live you better start flapping those big, fat lips of yours, Davy Boy."

"Okay. Okay. Wait! Wait a fuckin' second here! I've been shot for Christ's sake! Give me a moment."

I looked at my wristwatch. It still said the same time it did when I'd left the sanatorium yesterday morning.

"Fifty seconds."

"Okay. Okay, lemme think, here, will ya. The last time I saw her was October 7th. Yeah, that's right. October 7th. I picked her up from a farmer's market in Wilshire. Was gonna bring her out here to Palm Springs with me."

"So, where is she now?"

"I don't know."

"What do you fucking mean, you don't know?"

"I mean I didn't bring her. She got all mouthy and disrespectful. She started screaming and yelling at me. Crazy fuckin' bint."

"What about?"

"She tried to grift me, is what. She told me she was pregnant. She started trying to hit me up for some cash. For a scrape or something. I told her to take it down the arches. I told her it wasn't my fuckin' problem. She started mouthing off, yelling her big mouth off, so I kicked her outta my ride before we'd even left the L.A city limits. I left her ass at the side of the road."

"What are you talking about? A scrape? You mean an abortion?"

"Yeah, that's it. An abortion. She started trying to shake me down. Wanted cash. I told her it wasn't my fuckin' problem. I never blasted my load inside that whore. It wasn't my problem. I'd only let her suck me off at the end."

I felt a terrible pain in my chest then, a cold blade there.

And, then I did something I hadn't done since the war at Sugar Loaf Hill. I began to cry. My vision clouded over, the tears ran down my face and fell off my chin like a heavy rain. My right eye ached. Davy just looked at me, opened mouthed. First shocked, almost horrified and then he erupted into a cackling laughter.

"No, really?! This is priceless! Ya loved that little whore, didn't ya, Soldier Boy? Ya fell in love with her? I can't believe it, Soldier Boy cryin' over the whore he loved. Scott Kelly, the cold-blooded killer actually weepin' over a little whore. I wish the boys could all see ya now," he guffawed though his broken nose and the escaping air blew bubbles of blood.

I stumbled over to the bed again and took another fresh pillow in my fist. Tears still streaming down my face. A terrible pain in my chest and stomach that had nothing to do with consumption at all. I wept and I coughed. Davy stared at me, wild eyed, shaking his hands in the air, cowering.

"Wait! Wait! Fuckin' wait! I know where she went to. Jean, I know where she went! I know where she is. I'll tell ya where she is. Just wait."

I continued a swaying, dizzy shuffle towards him and he kicked out with his good leg trying to push himself back on his fat ass and gain some distance on the light blue carpet.

"A Doctor. She said she was going to see some doctor for the scrape. Some kraut doctor. A doctor Scott, she said. Doctor Scott or something."

I stopped. Frozen in a quick flash of memory. I remembered Jean and The Doc in the sanatorium that day, laughing together in the parking lot.

"Doctor *Schott*? Not a Doctor *Scott*?"

"Yeah, yeah, yeah. That's it. Some Doctor with a kraut name like that. Schott or Schmidt or somethin'. A kraut name, sure. He used to do scrapes to pay for his gambling debts. She was fuckin' him too, probably. He bought her things. Things with big price tags. Gifts, shit like that. She said he took her for rides in his Caddie, out to the coast. They watched the sunrise together and all that type of shit. He's got a wife and two kids, so I wanted her to blackmail him, get a grift goin', but she wouldn't. Dumb cooze. She said she was gonna go to him for the scrape. He works in some hospital for lepers or some shit in the city."

"Thanks, Davy Boy. You've been very helpful."

"You'll let bygones be bygones now, huh? I helped ya a lot today. Gave ya all the skinny on that whore of yours."

"No, Davy. This has been far too long a' coming. I was always gonna kill you," I picked up the pillow and stepped towards him. His face contorted into a sneering death mask.

"We laughed about ya, ya know? She thought you were a fuckin' joke with a little Irish cock. Fuckin' tiny. Like a baby's cock, she said. Scotty, the insecure little boy, beat the shit outta her when she tried to leave him. We fuckin' laughed about ya, ya dumb, mick fuck. She'd suck my cock and then Tony's cock, we'd laugh about ya and then she'd go and see ya in ya shitty little bar. She was a fuckin' whore and she laughed about ya, shit, we all laughed about ya. She played ya like a violin the whole time ya were together, ya fuckin' loser. She grifted you! She grifted ya good, ya fuckin' child killer. She was disgusted by ya. Like your wife and kid. Disgusted. And ya know what else? I knew that kid and woman were in the house. I knew it and ya did exactly what I thought ya'd do. Hell's got a special place for child killers like you, Soldier Boy!"

I put the pillow to his face, and he batted it away with hysterical hands.

"WAIT! Ya can't kill me! You'll be a dead man. They'll kill ya. They'll fuckin' kill ya! My LAPD guys, Mickey, the mob. They'll kill ya."

"How can they kill a man who's already dead?"

His eyes opened very wide; he'd finally understood.

"Give my regards to Benny when you see him."

I put the pillow over his face and shot him twice. Broke into a very deep coughing fit and collapsed onto the bed, hacking, and sobbing and screaming Jean's name silently into the emptiness of the room.

I didn't know how long had passed, but after a while I got

up and looked around the room for something that would tell me that Jean had been there. But there was nothing. I went to the bathroom, splashed cold water on my face, dried off with a soft hotel bath towel and drank water from the tap. I walked back into the main room and looked in the black leather briefcase again at the bundles of cash and then picked it up, returned the pistol to the small of my back, looked over at Davy.

"Hey Davy, you were right. That's what the Japs call Karma."

His corpse voided its bowels in retort as I left the hotel room and closed the door.

THE TOURISTS WERE still buzzing around the pool, drinking colorful cocktails, and chatting lazily to each other. I turned right and started walking down the terrace towards the stairs that would take me down to the first floor next to the swimming pool. As I tried to stroll casually down the last few steps, I glanced over towards the main entrance area with the flowers growing all over the wall and spotted the detective in brown walking towards me, probably on his way to Davy's room to split the dough. Fuck! At first, he didn't see me, he was too focused on the perimeter of the poolside area again. Constantly assessing for threats or looking for someone. I cursed my poor timing and tried to act cool, glancing at my stopped wristwatch like a businessman with an important meeting with a client that I was running late for. When I was close enough to smell his stale sweat and cheap cologne, he noticed me, his face automatically frowned into deep lines of suspicious recognition. He looked me up and down and then his eyes narrowed on the case in my hand. Shit! I had known it wasn't worth taking. I didn't know why I'd brought the damned thing with me. A final fuck you to Mickey Cohen and Anthony, maybe. The cop reached out, put his hand on my shoulder as I brushed roughly past him. I shook it off.

"Hey Mister, stop a moment." He was smart. He'd said it

just loud enough to gain everyone's attention around the pool without causing too much of a scene. Making sure there were witnesses. Trying to box me into a corner. Trying to cut off the ring. I carried on walking towards the main entrance and the parking lot. If I could get through the main gate and into the back alleys of Palm Springs, I would be okay. I could make it.

"Hey, Mister. Police! I said stop. STOP!" he dropped his hand on my shoulder again and as he did, I spun around, pulled the pistol from my back and let him have it in the gut two times. Point blank. He stumbled backwards clasping his red-soaked front and fell into the pool making a dull splash. The people milling around the water stopped and gasped in unison, the whole hotel took a deep breath and then two women screamed at different sides of the pool. I turned around again. I sped up my walking. Panting and puffing. Struggling to contain the hacks that were bucking in my chest and throat.

White wall fragments shattered, smashed, and cut into my face. The cop in the blue uniform wearing his cap now. On duty. Crouched on one knee on the gritty parking lot ground and firing at me the way they'd taught him in the academy. He fired again and I heard the smashing of glass behind me. I swung up my pistol and returned fire moving sideways as I squeezed off on the trigger. I missed him. My hand was shaking too erratically, I hit the car in front, to the left of him. He let off another shot and I felt it rip through the air by my head. I took my time and fired again, hitting him in the chest just below his badge. He crawled on his hands and knees towards a parked car and collapsed. I walked towards him and pulled the trigger on him again, but the pistol just *clicked, clicked, clicked*. Seven bullets per magazine. A rookie mistake and it could have cost me. I slipped out the clip, dropped it on the ground by his shiny black parade shoes and slid in a fresh clip. He rolled over on his back to get a look at my face. My eyes. I know he saw nothing there.

"Please," he mouthed it through a balloon of blood, and I shot him in the face.

Sirens now ripping the atmosphere in the distance apart,

echoing from a few blocks away. I stumbled through the black hotel gates that screamed 'THE DESERT INN' in gold and out onto the street, lurching and waving the gun and briefcase in my hands as I went. Shoppers on the street gawked, wailed, scrambled for cover in store entranceways and behind automobiles. I half ran, half fell down the pavement. The sirens were getting closer. I thought about Jean. I thought about dancing with her in my arms at the Chi-Chi Club, as though we were the only ones in the place. An engine roaring in my ears. The cops behind me. I thought about Jean. The roaring of the engine screeched beside me and I tried to swing my pistol up, but I was too weak. Too tired. I thought of Jean. I'd failed her.

"Boss, get the fuck in! Now!" Rudy shouted from the Rolls Royce. I leapt at the automobile, pulled open the door and fell inside. Rudy floored it. I swung the door shut and started to hack and hemorrhage, large thick pools of blood. Starting to pass out...

"No, don't you fuckin' pass out now! Hey! Hey! Wake the fuck up and help me out of here."

"I'm sorry. You weren't supposed to be here. You weren't supposed to be here. I'm sorry. I'm sorry..."

"WAKE THE FUCK UP!"

I opened my eyes; black curtains came down on the beach house and I was in the back of the Rolls again. It seemed like everything was bleeding. My insides. My mouth. My clothes. The dark leather seats. Slippery to the touch.

"Are you shot?" Rudy bellowed. I stared at the blood.

"Are you fuckin' shot?"

"No," I said, but I wasn't sure. I didn't think so. Sirens bombed through the air and echoed from building to building in the distance.

"The cops are on us! Fuck!"

"No, not yet. Keep driving. Carefully. Until we get out. Of the main strip. Then gun it. When you get to the. Desert road. Back to. Los Angeles. We are going. To be okay," I breathed heavy and tried to speak in between gasps like an asthmatic.

"Okay, Boss."

"We'll need to. Change cars. Soon as possible. Stop at the next diner or somewhere. With a few cars in. The parking lot. On the outskirts of town."

He quickly looked back at me and then at the briefcase.

"You talk to the girl? You got what was taken from you?"

"Yeah, maybe. But it isn't in the briefcase."

"So, what's in the case?"

"Half is yours. Your retirement fund, so you can get out and set your family up in New York. Or wherever. The other half is for my daughter."

"What are you talkin' about?"

I unclasped the briefcase with bloody fingers and coughed blood onto some of the cash bundles. The blood spread into the stacks of green paper like water marks.

His eyes widened and he just said, "Oh, shit."

"Rudy, do you know the Barlow Tuberculosis Sanatorium on the outskirts of the city?"

"What? Yeah, sure Boss, up by the ballpark, that's where my wife got her treatments. Why?"

"Take me there, please."

"Of course, whatever you say, Boss."

I slumped down in the back seat and tried to catch my breath. I thought about Jean and a thick, weighty, empty hopeless feeling filled my veins and arteries. I knew where she was and what had happened. I prayed I was wrong.

The Rolls Royce cruised out of the city limits and the sounds of sirens trailed off and remained within the confines of Palm Springs as we hit the desert road back to Los Angeles and the sanatorium, the place where it had all started. The words I had told Charlie at the bar the day before echoed in my mind and I whispered them aloud; "It's a never-ending circle of bullshit and blood…"

CHAPTER 10

THE SANATORIUM SURGED out of the damp ground and grew swollen as the automobile climbed the hill towards it. The red bricks were now colored black by the night and the yellow lights from the halls within leaked out onto the grounds beyond casting shadows across the jagged corrupted lawns.

I got out of the automobile and slammed the door. It sounded like mortar fire.

A telephone was ringing.

It started to rain again. Heavy rain. The rain grew fat on the rim of my helmet and fell. The ground liquified into shit and muck. My boots were sucked into the sludge.

I glanced back over to the automobile, but it was gone.

An old man with long grey hair in a raggedy brown suit and a shoulder holster was sprawled in the mud making a snow angel, he stopped and twisted his head, glaring over at me.

That was excessive, he said.

A telephone was ringing.

I looked at the sanatorium again. It was a smoking ruin. Snipers were crouched in the bell tower. Bullets cracked past my head and body. I stared up at their face; they were Jap soldiers with their skulls bashed in. I tried to return fire, but my hands were empty.

My Thompson machine gun was laid in a patch of yellow grass out of reach.

I had the taste of menstruation in my mouth again. I was beginning to savor the flavor and scent of it.

A telephone was ringing.

The sound of the Pacific Ocean crashing all around me, waves like drums. I ran towards the sanatorium, dodging and diving under broken trees and destroyed tanks.

A young, good-looking kid was trying to fix a smoking half-track, he grinned at me and pointed to the large gaping crater in his forehead,

It's a never-ending circle of bullshit and blood, he said.

A telephone was ringing.

My father was wearing a blue corduroy jacket, digging into the dirt, looking for mussels and cockles for our supper. He held bullet casings in his palms and showed them to me.

It's sink or fucking swim Boy, he said.

A telephone was ringing.

A little girl shivering, covered in muck and insects. She had the pneumonia and was trembling, holding out her hands to me, calling me *Daddy, Daddy, Daddy*. I told her I was sorry, but I didn't have any stories with happy endings, she wasn't supposed to have been there. She went to sleep with a bloody hole in her chest. I tried to hold her in my arms, but she went to New York with her mother. Every time I tried to hold her, she turned to shit and mud in my hands.

A telephone was ringing.

Jean was crying on my shoulder, she was wearing a long blue cotton dress, it had a maroon stain on the chest between her breasts.

It was the best birthday, she'd ever had.

I ran my hands around her hips and rested them on the small of her back. I slid two fingers deeply in and out of the moist hole there.

You're making me half-crazy and we're in public, she whispered.

Benny, Davy, two spics and a cop in a blue uniform were watching us dance with shadowy, crustified eye sockets from a table on the lawn. They drank from milk cartons and made grumbling comments. But I didn't care. They clapped their hands and cheered. Two Marines with no arms or legs shook their bloody, bug infested stumps at me. My mother cheered too, she was cutting a warm loaf of bread on the breakfast bar and clutching at her heart. Dark, yellow piss was pouring down her legs and puddling around her slippers.

A telephone was ringing.

Jean and I stood dancing to a song called Gloomy Sunday and I told her that I wanted her to have my baby.

Jean said she was waltzing Matilda.

I said, no, that was someone else, entirely.

A telephone was ringing.

It was my baby, I said.

She touched the crimson stain on her chest; *I'm too broken, Scotty*, she said. *I can't feel anything anymore, something is stuck*, she said.

She raised my wrist to my face and showed me the wristwatch, *do you see? Something is stuck*, she said.

We could get away from the sanatorium and find a new automobile and gun it away from Okinawa, I said.

We could get married, I said.

Let's retire in New York, I said.

But you're too broken, said Jean.

You don't love me, you just love the way I make you feel, she said.

What are you? A fucking psychiatrist? I said.

Fire ants are eating me from the inside out, but I could have a second chance with you, I said.

Why does my right eye ache? I asked.

A bullet through the fuckin' eye, Jean said.

What do the slant eyes call that? Karma, Soldier Boy? squealed Davy from the table in The Chi-Chi Club.

Benny looked up at me from over the Los Angeles Times and laughed, *Ha!*

Jean coughed blood and cried onto my shoulder.

I was the one who loved you most, she said.

Waltzing Matilda, she said.

I kissed Jean's lips softly, tasting the mud, the rot, and the death.

I couldn't eat and Charlie was cooking eggs sunny side up.

I wanna shoot dice, I wanna shoot my dice into a little Nip, said Charlie.

Why does my right eye always ache here? I asked.

So bright, it looked like a star going supernova, Jean said.

A telephone was ringing.

Someone in the crowd whistled loudly and a woman shouted out for Jean to get up.

I turned to face her. She wasn't there. I saw her standing on the roof of the crumbling sanatorium, holding the baby in her arms.

I tried to climb out of the Amphib, over the side, but my hands were too bloody, they slipped. I couldn't reach her. I told her to wait for me there, wait for me on the edge of the darkness. She leapt into the jagged ocean below grasping her daughter's hand. Disappearing into the black water and I sat alone in the diner.

ALONE IN THE booth. Someone had carved SHIT into the table. It was raining outside. It always seemed to be raining even when it wasn't. Rainwater. I could feel it pumping through my veins and arteries.

I never told you that I loved you. But I loved you, Jean. I really loved you. I should have said it, but I was too afraid. Now it's always too late to save you. Always too late to save us both.

Rudy slid back into the booth across from me. I tried to focus. Concentrate.

"Boss, you okay? You were pretty out of it for a while and you've been talkin' to yourself. I just went to take a piss. I'm sorry, I had to leave you on your own for a little while."

"Hey, is your buddy okay over there? He's been shouting and talking to himself," it was a big guy with a peppery mustache standing in the kitchen door, wearing a grease-stained, white apron and brandishing a spatula. The blue haired waitress from earlier in the day stood behind him, peering from around his meaty shoulder.

"Yeah, he's fine. He's just drunk. We had a stag party in Palm Springs today and we drank a lot. Too much."

"He looks like shit, if I'm honest about it, and Betty here said he's covered in what looks like blood."

"We got into a fight over a girl with another couple of fellas and that's why we had to leave the party early," laughed Rudy.

That seemed to satisfy Al's curiosity, he shook his head and chuckled. He and the blue haired waitress named Betty went back into the kitchen again, the door swinging back and forth behind them.

"You came back here?" I rasped.

"It's the only diner between Palm Springs and L.A. on this road, it looks like."

"How'd I get here. In the diner. In this booth, I mean?"

"I helped you walk in. Half-carrying you. You were talkin' a lot. But, not to anyone that I could see. Is there anything I can do, Boss?"

"We need to change automobiles," I croaked.

"There's an old blue Hudson parked outside. I'm guessin' it's the waitress, Betty's and she won't miss it until the end of her shift and then she'll probably get a ride with Al to the nearest cop shop. That'll buy us time. By the time she's realized that the Hudson's gone and told the cops, we'll be in L.A. long gone. I used to borrow automobiles from strangers in my more carefree days and Hudson's were my specialty. So, it'll be okay, I reckon."

"Good. That's great," I said.

The blue haired waitress, Betty brought a pot of hot coffee out of the kitchen and filled our cups.

"Are you okay, Sweetie?" she nodded and smiled down at me. She had the same eyes as the nurses in the sanatorium.

"Yes, Mam, I think I'll survive for the moment."

"Well, what doesn't kill you, only makes you stronger, I always say." I laughed out aloud to that, but she continued smiling like she'd not even noticed.

"Anything you need, you boys let me know. You're our only customers for the time being, due to the rain, maybe. So, give me a holler, okay?" she nodded her little, blue-flamed head at us both again and then went back into the kitchen.

"I looked in the briefcase. There's gotta be at least two or three hundred thousand dollars in it. I've never seen so much dough."

"Where is it now?"

He hefted it up from beside him, flashed the black leather over the tabletop and then settled it back down on the seat beside him.

"Where'd it come from, Boss?"

"Davy and three LAPD cops stole heroin from Mickey Cohen, sold it to people in New York and that's the cash from the business transaction or some of it anyway," I said.

"Shit! So, it's Mickey Cohen's dough?"

"No, it's our fucking dough now. Mickey doesn't know they sold the junk; and all, but one of the people who the cash belongs to is dead."

"There's one more of them still alive?"

"Yeah, maybe one more cop, but I guess he's still in Palm Springs or wherever. Fuck him. He won't be bothering you. His friends are dead, Davy's dead. You're safe."

"Yeah, but what about Mickey Cohen and Tony?"

"Mickey and Anthony will blame me for snuffing Davy, that means you'll have time to get your family outta L.A. By the time they have both realized what's happened, you'll be outta their reach and living the high life far away from all this bullshit. But it's a risk, Rudy. If you take the briefcase you've gotta take everything that comes with it. You'll always have to look over your shoulder if you take it. It's not too late to back out now."

Rudy closed his eyes for a moment, nodded and then gave me a hard look.

"I'll take my chances. I wanna get my family away from this life and give them better than I ever had. I think I'm gonna take the money and run. What about you?"

"I'm staying here in L.A. I have a few more things I need to do. I just want you to give me your word that you'll give my half of the cash to my daughter. I'm trusting you, Rudy."

"You'll be able to give it to her yourself, if you run too."

"Rudy, look at me. I can barely walk and even if I could run, I wouldn't. The briefcase is your responsibility now. Take your family and get out of L.A. Get outta this life. It's poison and it slowly poisons everyone and everything in it. Please just give me your word that you'll get the money to my daughter. It's her inheritance. Please."

"I'll get my family to New York and the first thing I'll do is look up your daughter and give her your half. I swear it."

I nodded and we chinked our coffee cups in a toast. The waitress Betty came out of the kitchen again.

"You two hell raisers decided what you'd like to eat?"

"Apple pie," we both said.

"And a carton of milk," said Rudy grinning.

"I'm sorry, I don't quite follow," said the waitress.

"It's a private joke from a story I told him about. Don't worry about it," I said.

The waitress flashed the same smile and went back into the kitchen. A few moments later brought out the slices of apple pie. Rudy ate quickly, spooning the pastry into his wide mouth. I picked at mine slowly and just sipped at my coffee, trying not to cough, trying not to pass out. My body felt as though I'd been swimming in the ocean for days. Drained. Every movement was an exhausting effort.

Rudy and I talked a little more here and there and were about to get up and get ready to leave when the bell above the door jingled again and a man came in holding a rag over the chrome door handle. He wore a tan trench coat darkened and slick with rain over a charcoal grey suit. An unusual looking man, tall with a creamy face, blonde foppish hair dampened by the rain and a mustache with the tips waxed up at the ends like a sideshow magician. There was something familiar about him that I couldn't quite place. He reminded me of someone. He casually glanced with stale grey eyes at Rudy and me and then went to the booth directly behind us. Stood looking down at the table for a minute, twitched and then slowly wiped down the leather seating with the rag and then wiped the tabletop down too. He slid into the booth carefully, wiping his hands on the rag, then wiped down the surface of the table again and then placed the rag neatly on the table to his left, then readjusted it to his right. He knew Rudy and me were watching him and didn't seem to care; too preoccupied with his manic rituals.

Betty came out of the kitchen sunnily and went over to take his order.

"Good afternoon, Hon. What'll it be?"

The magician ran a hand through his floppy, blonde hair like it was another one of the rituals.

"Do you have paper cups?" he said with an accent that, like his face, seemed familiar, but was unplaceable. A British accent that had been long ago Americanized. A hint of Boston.

"Paper cups?"

"Yes, paper cups, Madam. You know the kind that you'd use at a party, say. The kind you'd dispose of after using. A cup that is made of paper. A paper cup."

"Erm, I'm not sure. I think so. Like a cup for a to-go order you mean?"

"Yes, that's right, like in a takeaway order. I'd like a coffee, black, two teaspoons of sugar, in one of those paper cups. Please."

"Erm, okay, anything else?"

"No, I should think not. Not yet anyhow," he ran his hand through his damp hair again trying to keep it from hanging into his face and then wiped his hands on the rag roughly. Twitched. Betty went back to the kitchen, cringing and raising an eyebrow at Rudy and I as she passed by.

"That magician guy is highly strung." said Rudy

"Yeah," I agreed, running my hand to the small of my back, but my pistol wasn't there.

"Where's my pistol, Rudy?" I said hushed.

"The pistol? It fell out of your jacket when I was liftin' you outta the Rolls. So, I tucked it under one of the back seats outta sight. If it fell out again in here it would have been a big problem, I thought."

"A.B.C, Rudy. Remember that for later. Etch it into your memory."

"What's that mean?"

"Always. Be. Carrying."

"You think this klumniks a threat?" he hooked a thumb in

the direction of the booth behind him.

"Yeah, possibly. I don't know. When you've been in this life long enough anyone and everyone seems like a possible threat. But there's definitely something familiar about him. Maybe, he was with the Boston Mob a while ago. I'm not sure. Maybe, it's nothing."

The waitress brought out the pot of coffee and a paper cup and placed them in front of the man.

"Thank you, Madam," he poured the coffee into the paper cup.

"Where's the sugar, please?"

"Oh, I'll just go and fetch it," said the waitress.

"And could you ask the cook to come out here. I have a complaint I'd like to make."

"Oh, is everything okay?"

"I'd like to see the cook or the owner of the establishment, whomever is in the kitchen sweating over the grill. Right away, now, if you would be so kind, Madam."

The waitress hurried into the kitchen cringing again. There was a harried moment of whispering and then Al came out of the kitchen for the second time that day, grasping the same spatula, looking surly with the waitress next to him.

"I heard there was a problem, friend?" said Al.

"Yes, are you *the* Al of Al's All-American Diner?"

"Yeah, I be he. What seems to be the problem, Mister?"

"Well, Al this table was sticky when I came in and sat down. Sticky. It's rather quite unpleasant. Sticky like an insect's legs or something quite unpleasant like that. Can you imagine? Sticky. A sticky table. It's quite unpleasant. It's quite unpleasant. It's quite unpleasant."

Al and the waitress looked at each other, mutually thinking that the guy was a certified fruitcake and then Al's head exploded in a spray of red. Betty the waitress just had enough time to let out a shocked yelp before her blue-colored head snapped back in a bloody mist as well. They lay tumbled together on the black and white tiled floor in an awkward heap. The magician was stood then, next to Rudy and me, a Smith and Wesson .38 policeman's service revolver in each hand. He'd killed the old couple with a headshot each, moved fast, with skill and experience. The magician was a certified hard case, for sure.

"That was regrettable, but I do despise the American roadside dining experience. These shabby little places in the middle of nowhere catering to the filthy, huddled crowds," he said, lurching at the end of our booth and pointing one revolver at me and another at Rudy.

"It's a possibility that you both might be sharp enough to theorize what it is that I want, Gentlemen. Though, not sharp enough to hide a getaway vehicle as conspicuous as a Rolls Royce," he tittered.

"You're the third cop, Davy had on his payroll," I said.

He twitched. Winking convulsively.

"Davy was on *my* fucking payroll. *Mine.* Not the other way around. The piece of shit worked for me. Are you the one from The Desert Inn?"

"Yeah, that'll be me," I said.

"You killed my associates. However, it works out to my advantage, because I was going to take the whole caboodle for myself and then kill them all anyhow. The fuckheads had exceeded their usefulness and had caught on to me. You did me a favor. Someone I love is in a very bad spot and I need that money. You've helped me more than you know. Thank you very much. Bravo."

"Well, I'm happy I could provide a service."

"Yes, how very humorous. Your face looks familiar. Have we met?" he was looking at me closely, frowning. Scrutinizing.

"No, I think I would have remembered you and you definitely would have remembered me," I replied.

"No, we have met. You're Jimmy Kelly, are you not?"

"It's Scott Kelly."

"Yes, I knew I recognized the face as soon as I walked in this filthy pit. Time hasn't been very kind to you at all though, I must say."

I just nodded.

"Salt Lake City, February 1946, now that was a bloodbath and a half. That place ruined me, Kelly. Fucking ruined me," he frowned, stared off dreamily.

"Yeah, it was my first real job," I said and sipped at my coffee to stifle a cough.

"Yes, it showed, I'm afraid to say. You went in all guns blazing like some kind of a cowboy. Killed everyone in the fucking hotel except the filthy fucks you should have killed. Even killed the maids, I heard. Rather quite amateurish and cringeworthy actually."

"I'm here now though, ain't I?"

"Very true. Not a lot of people made it out of the Peery hotel. A lot of fucking cockroaches did but not a lot of people. You must be surprised to see me up and around again with such pep in my stride?"

"You guys know each other?" Rudy hissed to me.

"I thought I'd killed him a few years back in Salt Lake City," I said.

"I'm here now though, ain't I?" the magician said imitating me in a mocking tone. He turned his attention to Rudy then.

"He shot me in the back, like a coward in the night. Quite dishonorable. No hard feelings though. Salt Lake City wasn't exactly an honorable job for any of us. I sold my soul in that hotel. My fucking soul. The filthy Beetle Man took my soul. I couldn't save the kid. Couldn't save myself. Salary was certainly something though. I came to Los Angeles to try and start afresh but they dragged me back into the filth and the darkness. And now here you and I are again at the end of our stories," he looked back at me, "isn't it uncanny how all paths diverge, but then intersect once more later on? Fate. Karma."

"It's all a circle of bullshit."

"Yes, that's quite profound observation, Kelly. I have to say that I agree. A circle of bullshit, indeed."

I slurped my coffee slowly to show that I was done with any more conversation.

The magician grimaced and took the cue. Slid one of the revolvers into the pocket of his trench coat, keeping the barrel of the other revolver pointed at me, then stepped back slowly to his booth and picked up the rag and threw it at Rudy.

"What do you want me to do with this?" Rudy asked.

"Use it to wipe down the briefcase, showing special attention to the handle and the grooves around the handle."

Rudy slack-jaw gawked at me. I looked back. Shrugged. Rudy started to slowly wipe down the case, shaking his head as he did it.

The man shook his revolver in my direction. "You, Kelly, stand up and go over there behind the register and take out the cash. I'll need to make this look like a robbery gone awry."

"You think I'm going to help you set up the crime scene? Get the fuck outta here. I'd rather die in this booth."

He turned his attention quickly to Rudy. "You, Fat Man, wipe that briefcase handle again."

"Huh? I only just finished wipin' the fuckin' thing."

"Yes, but then you touched it again with your fingers, contaminating it again. Wipe it thoroughly and put it on the floor here, holding it by the handle using the rag, fuck head. Holding the handle with the rag. The rag. Holding the handle with the rag."

It looked as though the magician was beginning to come undone. His twitching had escalated, into jerks and spasms.

"This fakakte guy's not all there. He's one of them obsessive clean freaks," whispered Rudy.

I could feel myself beginning to come undone as well. Didn't try to stifle the coughs. I started hacking and opened the flood gates. The magician's eyes bulged, and he jumped back away from our booth.

"Stop that! What the fuck is wrong with you people?! Cover your mouth with your fucking hand when you cough and then sterilize your hand! What's that? Is that... is that blood? What the fuck is wrong with you, Kelly?!" he shook the revolver at me and shouted.

"He's got the consumption," said Rudy.

"What? Tuberculosis?" he almost screamed it, semi hysterical.

"I'm in the final stages of Tuberculosis now, Englishman. You might as well shoot me, put me outta my misery, because I'm already dead for all practical purposes." I coughed and spat more droplets of blood onto the table surface. Put my fingertip in the blood and wrote my name.

"Here lies one whose name was writ in blood," I said, winking at him.

The magician in the trench coat took a few more steps back, twitches erupted in his face and shoulders. He held the revolver shaking on me. Rudy wiped the bloody tabletop with the magician's rag.

"Fuck! Fuck! What the fuck are you doing?! Stop that! This instant! Please! I need that money! Give me the briefcase now!" he bellowed. Full hysterical. His face had flushed almost purple and sweat was suddenly dripping down his face. Rudy continued wiping the tabletop smearing the blood into the surface.

"STOP IT I SAY!" screeched the magician.

Rudy flung the rag into his face. The magician's shrieks were the worst I'd ever heard. Worse than anything I'd heard on the island of Okinawa. He caught the rag full in the face and wrestled with it as though it were a wild animal mauling him. The high-pitched screaming rattled the windows. The revolver clattered to the tiled floor. Rudy quickly slid out of the booth, leapt, slammed into the magician's chest, tackling him to the ground. A quarterback footballer.

I crawled out of the booth towards the revolver spinning slowly on the floor, its dark wooden handle reflecting the diner's lighting. Rudy and the magician struggled together on the black and white tiles. The sound of shoe heels squealing, echoes of gym class many years ago. The magician was wailing, fully hysterical and clawing at Rudy's face, pulling his hair. A tortured kind of screaming that escaped his mouth. I collapsed to the floor, reached the revolver, brandished it in my hand, as the magician stuck his thumb into Rudy's eye and threw him off of him. Scrambling to his feet and fumbling in his trench coat pocket for the other revolver, while wiping his lower face erratically with the back of his hand. He was completely focused in his rage and madness, directing it all at Rudy, who was still splayed on the floor holding his eye in pain. I pointed the revolver, palsied, squeezed on the trigger and let off a shot. The shot went wide smashing into the diners' entrance doors, shattering glass. The magician ducked, reached into the pocket of his trench coat, and ripped out the revolver. I fired again and the shot went wide again, ripping apart some shuttered blinds. The magician snapped off a shot and I felt floor tiles explode next to my ear, deafening me momentarily. I tried to focus my breathing. Counting backwards. Jean's face. My daughter's face. I squeezed down on the trigger, the revolver barked and spat, hitting the magician in the chest. He fell back sprawling into a booth. His legs sticking out ridiculously.

Rudy got up, slipping to his feet, snatched the briefcase from our booth and then helped me up from the floor. We hustled out of the diner's front doors together; the glass fell jingling out of the frame, a standing ovation as it slammed shut again.

THE RAIN PELTING down in sheets. The parking lot had turned into rivers and pools of grey water, set on blood colored fire by the flashing of the fluorescent sign above the diner.

Rudy started towards the cop's car, a black 1945 Dodge. I let him go on, waving him away and I stumbled over to the Rolls, opened the door and retrieved my Colt from under the back seat. Pointed the pistol towards the rear left tire and shot into the rubber tread, the wheel exploded exposing the skeleton of the rim and I dragged myself over to the waitresses blue Hudson and repeated the action on its front left tire.

"What are you doin'?" Rudy yelled over to me as he swung the briefcase into the backseat of the Dodge and then swung himself into the front seat. I fell in beside him on the passenger side soaked with rain.

"Just in case," I said.

"Just in case what?" he said.

"We didn't finish him. Remember you've always gotta finish them to be certain."

He started to fiddle with the underneath of the ignition area, but then chuckled. "He left the keys in here. Limey schmuck," he said, turning the key in the ignition and gunning the engine.

"Some luck at last," I said.

Then the rear windows glass erupted, and shards flew.

"Shit! I knew it. That fucking guy has more lives than a cat. Get us outta here, Rudy."

Another bullet exploded through the rear window again splintering the windshield. The magician was stood slouched against the Hudson outside of the diner's entrance bloody and howling into the heaving waves of rain. A mad man drenched in blood and water. Rudy gunned the engine again. Rubber squealed. We sped away. Pursued by more screams, howling and bullets as we skidded out of the diner parking lot and back onto the road to L. A. once more.

"Who the fuck was that, Boss?" Rudy finally asked, staring through the cracked windshield at the grey wet road.

"An old friend, I'd forgotten I had, I guess."

"Shit, talk about coincidences, huh?"

"Yeah, but I've got a feeling you'll be seeing him again, Rudy. Watch your back from here on out."

"What? Are you fuckin' serious?"

"It's a possibility. A man as sick and obsessive as that? Who the fuck knows?"

"That poor old couple back in the diner. They didn't deserve to go out like that."

"Casualties of war, unfortunately," I shrugged.

"What war? They died for nothin'."

"They were casualties of the war you've found yourself in. You're a bona fide hard case now, Rudy. There's no going back for you now. You're in a war."

"And you? What about you? Your war?"

"That's coming to an end tonight."

We both went back to saying nothing. Rudy drove, both hands ghostly, gripping the steering wheel to stop the shakes he was trying to hide. I stared out of the window into the rain. It wasn't yet sunset, but the sky was bruised by the clouds and the diminishing sun. Darkness was coming down fast, a final curtain. My right eye ached. The rain pelted the roof, the windshield, and the ground ahead. Finally going home to Jean.

FORTY-FIVE MINUTES hadn't passed before we saw the lights in the dimness behind. Two yellow eyes, wide with madness and swinging all over the moist gloom behind. Rudy put his foot down on the accelerator and I checked the clip in my pistol. Four rounds remained. Four was the number of death in Okinawa. Unlucky. I coughed into the crook of my arm. Tasted blood. Glanced into the rearview. The headlights were gaining on us. Stalking. Rudy was grimacing, his teeth clenched together, a man in pain.

"Pull over to the side of the road. We've gotta finish this."

"I can outrun him, Boss. We can lose him in L.A."

"And then what? I should have finished him in the diner. It was a rookie mistake. No. Pull over, Rudy. He's got a bullet in the chest and probably one left in the chamber of his revolver, if I counted right and if he doesn't carry extra. He'll be woozy from blood loss and half crazy. I'll just put him down quick and easy then we'll get outta here. I coughed onto my pistol and saw small droplets of maroon and phlegm pooled on the barrel. I swallowed the pulpy blood back down. My right eye ached deeper than ever. A star going supernova.

"This is fuckin' bullshit. Maybe it ain't him."

"It's him. It's *always him*. Pull over, get out. Go out into the sticks and shrubbery, lie down and wait. When he pulls in behind me, circle round him from the side. Don't get behind him or you'll catch one of mine. You understand?"

"Yeah, I got it."

He swerved over to the side of the road. Switched off the ignition. I passed him the Magician's .38 and he took it with a clenched jaw. Checked the chamber gingerly.

"There's only one bullet left."

153

"Hopefully, that's all you're gonna need. Now go."

He swung his heavy body out of the Rolls and jogged off disappearing into the dusk. I hacked a few times onto my fist, wheezed and eyeballed the rearview. Watching the orbs of light grow larger, illuminating everything around it, painting everything an awful taint of sickly yellow. I didn't expect Rudy to pull a trigger. I just wanted him out of the way. I glanced at the briefcase of cash on the backseat of the Rolls, lit by the Magician's automobile behind. The sound of an engine was deafening and for a split second I was back in an Amphib' heading back to the empty beaches of Okinawa. My daughter's face in candlelight. Jean's face in white sheets. I forced my weight against the door. Then an atomic explosion of tearing steel and crushed metal and darkness.

CHRISTMAS DAY 1947… Jean's throat underneath my mouth. Nat King Cole singing 'The Christmas Song' on the wireless radio. Jean flowed underneath and against me, a soft current. Her long hair spread over the pillow, water on sand. She held me tightly. Her bare neck, sweet and soft. I ran my tongue over its nakedness, felt her tendons tighten. My hands ran smoothly over her goose bumped flesh, over her hardened dark nipples, I squeezed. Her naked neck. My hands and fingers clamped around her throat. Her naked throat. Squeezed. She gripped my wrists with her small hands. Squeezed. Her eyes searched for mine, but my eyes were on the emptiness underneath my grip. I was close and I squeezed again. She bucked her body underneath mine, it heightened my pleasure, the depth of the feeling. I squeezed harder and Jean gasped, drowning in me. I finished inside her and my eyes finally found hers lost in the brightness of the window. I eased myself out of her and rolled off. She was quiet for a long time. She rolled her head and stared at the ceiling. She sighed. I breathed heavily, catching breaths. Nat King Cole still sang about Christmas on the radio and finally, she spoke.

"Scotty, what was that?"

"What was what?" I said, lighting a cigarette and blowing smoke towards the ceiling she was staring at.

"You know what."

"I don't, Jean."

"You were hurting me. You wouldn't stop. I wanted you to stop. I don't like those kinds of things. And you finished inside me even though I always beg you not to. Why?"

"I don't know. I thought you liked it."

"No, I didn't. I was trying to get you off of me, Scott. Why do you have to be so rough with me sometimes?"

"Where's the necklace?"

"Huh?"

"The necklace? That I gave you. For your birthday. You're not wearing it. Where is it?"

"Huh? The necklace?"

"The fucking diamond necklace, Jean? Where is it?"

"I didn't want it to get broken, so I took it off, Scotty. It's at home in my jewelry box. What's that got to do with anything?

"You're fucking someone else, aren't you?"

"What?! What? No, of course not, Scotty. How'd you even come to that conclusion?

"Where is it? I thought it meant something to you. I know there's someone else, Jean. There always is. Isn't there?

"Do we really have to have this conversation again, Scott? It's Christmas Day for crying out loud. Is that why you were so rough? Because I wasn't wearing the fucking necklace? Jesus Christ, Scott."

"Are you fucking someone else? You took off the necklace when you fucked him, right?"

"Scott, this is delusional lunacy, I'm leaving. I'm not staying here for this. I've put up with too much of this kind of shit. I'm not staying here for this. I'm really not."

She slid out of the bed and walked naked towards the chair with her clothes hanging there.

"Where the fuck do you think you're going? You're staying right here, Jean. You're staying right here, and we are going to have a nice Christmas Day together!"

"Please, Scotty. I want to go. I can't stay here now. I want to leave. I don't want to fight with you. Not today. I'm tired, Scotty. I'm really tired."

My anger cannibalizing itself and breeding. I leapt from the bed and punched the wall beside her head. She screamed and cowered. My hand throbbed, powdered with dust and plaster.

"You're fucking staying here, Jean. You think you can play me like a fool? I know where you're going? Do you think I'm a fool? Do you think I'm a fucking idiot? Do you?"

"Please, Scott! You're really scaring me. You're really frightening me. This isn't you. This isn't you, Scott. This is your mental problems from the war. I love you but you need help. You need help, Scott. Please, Scott. Please let me leave."

"So, you can run away to him?"

"Who? There isn't anyone else, Scott."

"You're not leaving me, Jean. You're not leaving me too. You're not deserting me too!"

"There's no one else, Scott. Please. I just want to go home."

A WOMAN SCREAMED. The screams were high pitched and agonized, the shocked kind.

CHRISTMAS DAY. My fists clenched and unclenched. Jean screamed. It was Christmas, 1947 and I smashed the day apart with a wine bottle. I took the bottle and my fists to everything, to the walls, the furniture. To Jean. And afterward alone in the shattered remains of my house, I took the broken glass to my own face. Stabbing and slicing. Scarring. Hating myself.

A WOMAN SCREAMED. The screams were high pitched and agonized, the shocked kind.

I FELT RAIN falling on my face. I couldn't breathe. Gasping. The sound of metal clicking, creaking and rain fall on grit. Opened my eyes with effort. Didn't know where I was. Saw early evening stars in a sky that was the color of bruises. The woman screamed again. I coughed up blood and swallowed it back down. The Dodge crumpled and crushed from the back end. My legs underneath the passenger side, my body on the road, the passenger door swung open. I tried to sit up. My body too heavy, smashed back down by the waves of rain. I rolled my head in the grit to look at the other automobile conjoined to the wreckage of the Dodge. My pistol lay near the rear wheel out of use and out of reach.

A blonde woman with a red painted face was in the front passenger seat of the other automobile, a large piece of glass was speared through her shoulder and she was fingering it with bloody fingertips and shrieking again and again from a black hole in the face of crimson.

My eyes flicked to a flash of white, a naked thing that crawled around from the back of the wreckage on all fours. It slithered up the passenger door, a horrific red, pink, and white spider. It hissed in tongues to the woman. Grasped the shard of glass and slid it out of her shoulder as she wept and moaned. I watched from a hundred miles away as the spider-like creature plunged the glass knife into the woman's throat again and again. The sound too wet, a cough, sucking, gurgling I'd heard many times. The woman drowned in her own blood, the noises ceased as abruptly as they had started and all I could hear was the rain. The naked spider slapping its hands into the soggy road, crawling towards me and speaking in tongues. Its facial features masked by hair that hung in tangled strands, a gaping gash gasping and hemorrhaging blood on its bony upper chest. I tried to get up. Couldn't. The thing clambered over to me slowly. It spoke in tongues, giggling and weeping at the same time.

"1946, upon the Peery stair, I met the Beetle Man who wasn't there! He wasn't there again today, oh how I wish, I wish he'd go away! I loved you, Li Yu. I couldn't save you.

They were fucking little children there. And what have I become? Now, I am become Death. You promised, Mother. 1946, upon the Peery stair, I met a man who wasn't there."

It sounded like a poem I'd heard when I was very young and now the creature uttered it repeatedly like a soothing mantra, the shard clasped in its fist. The blood and glass capturing the moonlight. The thing prowled over to me and raised the knife of glass into the space above my chest still muttering its murder mantra, then it froze, twisted its head towards my Colt. It slid back and snatched it up quickly, giggling and held it limply pointed towards my eye. Jarring my memory.

Rudy stepped out from around the front of the Dodge and shot the creature point blank in the face, its features bucked and exploded. I was showered in pieces of tooth and bone. The creature shriveled up into a ball, kicked out its legs, twitched and then stopped. Still. Rudy stopped too. He stood shaking, in shock, staring down at the ugly naked corpse.

"Rudy? Rudy? Rudy!?"

"Yeah?"

"You okay?"

"Yeah."

"Help me up, would you? Rudy? Help me up."

But he didn't, he just collapsed down onto his knees next to me in the rain staring at the crushed automobile.

"What the fuck was he naked for?"

"Who the hell knows? You think the Dodge will still run?"

"We won't know unless we try. You hurt?"

"No, I think I'm okay. Except the consumption. That wasn't knocked out of me," I tried to laugh but even the fake kind had finally failed me. Rudy's face remained fixed on the Dodge. After a moment he nodded to himself slightly and then helped me up. I retrieved my pistol from the creature's dead grasp, and we got into the Dodge, soaking wet, listening to the rain attacking the roof.

"I had to kill him, right, Boss?"

"There was no other way about it, Rudy. You saved my life.

What's left of it anyhow."

Rudy just nodded slowly again, then repeated the action as if trying to convince himself of something. He ran his fingers through his wavy hair and tried the ignition. The Dodge rattled to life.

"You've got the luck of the Irish, Boss. I'll give you that."

"You reckon it'll get us to where we are going?"

"So long as no cops pull us over, I think we are goin' to be able to get where we're both goin'."

"Yeah, I've got the luck of the Irish," I said, but hacked into my palsied hand, staring at the black blood smeared there, I wondered who I was still trying to shine on.

CHAPTER 11

IT HAD STOPPED raining as the shroud of twilight darkened completely over the valleys and the roads of L.A. The streets back to the sanatorium were shiny, wet, and cloaked in a welcoming gloom. The moistened air helped my breathing and I had the shattered remains of the window of the wrecked Dodge wound down, inhaling the soaked Californian evening air. Rudy occasionally pawed at his bruised, swollen eye, cursing to himself and listening to the radio, but switched it off once the news reports started shouting about the shoot-outs in Palm Springs and the diner. I sat listening to my own harried breathing and the clunking of the Dodge willing itself to the finish line. I knew how the automobile felt. Almost at the end of our story. Jean and me.

Jean. She wasn't at the sanatorium. I already knew that she wouldn't be there, but listening to my wheezing lungs, I tried praying for the first time since Okinawa.

THE SANATORIUM'S ROOMS were lit up in places and from the passenger seat of the Dodge, I could see nurses pacing to and fro in the windows that were yellow and bright. It was nearly eight thirty, some of the patients in Ward B would've had their baths by now and be back in their bunks, reading until lights out at nine thirty. The Doc would be finishing his hospital rounds, desk work and would leave to go home at around nine o'clock, if he weren't meeting any of the nurses for overtime that night.

The automobiles engine spluttered smoke and I placed my hand on Rudy's shoulder.

"Well, the Dodge made it. This is my final stop, Rudy."

He stared ahead, nodded. I saw tears in his eyes and pretended I hadn't noticed.

"At least, you're somewhere where you can get help now, Boss," he said.

"Yeah, I think everything's going to be okay now, Rudy. Everything will be okay. I won't be able to get to New York any time soon though, so remember your promise." More lies.

"Okay, I won't forget. You've got my word. I'll give your half of the money to your daughter as soon as I arrive in New York, before I even look at the Empire State. I'll place it in her hands myself. By the way, what's her name? Your daughter, I mean, I don't think you ever mentioned it."

"Matilda. Her name's Matilda." I could say it without it triggering any bad memories then. It came as a relief to say her name after so long. Like admitting a truth, an insecurity, a fear to a good friend after years suffering alone with it.

"Pretty name."

"It is. Thank you, Rudy. Thanks for everything. After, I get out of the sanatorium and I'm back into fighting condition, send me a postcard from where you are, and I'll come and visit you out there." One final mistruth.

"Really? That would be great, Boss."

"Sure, send the postcard to my bar. I'll be there. You think the Dodge will get you near to your house?"

"Yeah, I'll get nearby to home and then ditch it somewhere. Scott, mazel tov."

We nodded at each other finally and shook hands. I passed him a piece of paper with my daughter's address scribbled on it. He read it in the beam of the moonlight, folded it and slipped it into his pocket. I got out of the Dodge, slammed the door, and stood watching as the surviving rear light of the Dodge grew dim and then faded completely in the California twilight. I wondered how Rudy would get on. A briefcase full of dough, a large family in tow and maybe Mickey Cohen's soldiers not far behind. I wished him all the luck in the world. He'd need it now. He'd need a lot more.

I turned towards the parking lot and walked slumped,

stooped over, and wheezing to The Doc's Cadillac in the somber October night air. It shone in the moonlight, inviting me in. I gazed in the driver's side window; empty except for my own reflection in a black mirror. A wraith peering back at me, lost and unsure of where to go, unable or unwilling to leave purgatory. I opened the door and slid smoothly in and then onto the rear black leather seats. Smelling Jean's Chanel number 5 soaked into the very pores of the automobile. I heaved and spluttered into my stinking, clotted rag, waiting for The Doc to show up. Closed my eyes. Felt Jean's lips on mine and her fingers gently stroking the skin of my cheeks just under my eyes. Could feel her breath on my face and feel our bodies sinking into each other's. Her long hair falling over my hands. So many damn things I wanted to say to her. Needed to say to her. But, when the driver's door of the Cadillac slammed shut and I opened my eyes, Jean was gone and I knew then, what I had always really known in my heart. Jean was gone for keeps and she'd always been gone for keeps. She'd never even been there from the beginning and we'd both just been ghosts the entire time. Just echoes of lives we'd never really lived. A cycle of repetitive dreams and confused hallucinations in a dying man's mind.

"Hey Doc, no hot dates with any of the hot little nurses tonight?" I hissed, stabbing the pistol into the nape of his neck.

He slowly placed both of his hands on the steering wheel and gripped it tightly, the same way Rudy had done. His Adam's apple went up and down. He smelt like hand sanitizer, sweat and antiseptic.

"Hello, Mr. Kelly, I was wondering when you would show up again. You could say I've been waiting for you. Waiting for this."

"I'm not here for any treatments. This is the End Stage, Doc. End. Stage."

"Of that, I am well aware, Mr. Kelly," I noticed he had dropped the word "Sport" from his vocabulary once I had a pistol stuck in his neck.

"Put the key in the ignition and drive."

"To where, may I ask?"

"Take me to the place you use to take Jean."

"Yes… Yes. Very well. I understand," he murmured, started the automobile and drove slowly out of the sanatorium parking lot, down towards the city and I guessed out to a coastal road. I kept the pistol firmly above his white shirt collar as he drove. Pulled myself up closer to him as I spoke.

"Don't try anything smart, Doc. I'm sure, being a man of medical science, you understand what a bullet would do to your vertebrae at this range."

"Yes, it's quite all right. I wasn't going to try anything funny, as you say. I knew this would happen and I've been expecting it. Waiting for it. Jean told me what kind of a man you are. So, I knew after you'd left the hospital, that you'd come back for me sooner or later. Perhaps, I might have been hoping that you'd be too sick, but, well, you're here now. Jean doubted it, but she must have meant something very much to you, after all."

"I loved her, Doc. I never told her that, but I did. I loved her."

"So, did I."

"What did you say?"

"I said, I loved her too."

I pushed the pistol harder into the flesh of his spine, biting my bottom lip until I tasted fresh blood.

"Say that again!" I cocked the pistol audibly.

"I said, I loved her. I was utterly intoxicated by her since the first time I laid my eyes on her. I had a good life. I have two children, a wife, and a house in the suburbs, but I was infatuated with Jean. She infatuated me, Kelly. I'd never met a woman who'd made me feel, so, I don't know, alive, somehow all powerful. I saw her the first time she'd come to the hospital to see you and we had spoken briefly in the reception area that day. I couldn't get her out of my mind after that first meeting. I can't explain it. There was something about her. Something that positively illuminated from her. That's the real reason I let you use my office the second time she visited you, I was hoping at the time, it would give me an opportunity, a way for her to see me, the office, I mean, would be a chance of some kind of a conversation starter. It sounds positively demented; I am well aware. I waited in the parking lot that day for her. Pretending I needed some medical papers from my Cadillac and timed it precisely so that I'd make my way back into the hospital when I had seen she was coming out. That's how it started and once it had started, I was too weak for her to make it stop. I was too weak…"

A cop car, siren blaring and blazing roared past us in the opposite direction. I removed the pistol from his neck, waited for the cop car to disappear and then put the barrel back and he nodded, accepting, continuing his confession.

"Jean and I, it started slowly, almost tentatively, then it escalated so rapidly. She started coming to my office after lights out when you and the other patients were asleep, and we would make love in my office. I'd drive her out to see the ocean. She loved the sound of the Pacific at night."

I couldn't see his face, but from the wavering in his voice I knew he had started sobbing as he drove. My own vision blurry. My face wet. He drove down a quiet coastal road only lighted by the moonlight and the beams of the yellow light coming from the Cadillac's headlights. The Doc pulled into a roadside picnic area that overlooked Santa Monica Pier and the Pacific Ocean and switched off the engine. We sat in silence for a while listening to the waves crashing below. The sound of it made me remember L-Day in Okinawa, but no relapses or repeats came into my mind.

"She's dead, isn't she, Doc?" I asked, but it was more of a statement of fact. I already knew Jean was dead.

"Yes, she's dead," he whispered and let out a moan, sobbing again. Heavier. "She's gone," he cried. I took the pistol away from his neck and rested it in my lap.

"What happened to her?"

"It was an accident, of course. But I killed her all the same."

"How?"

"Towards the end of September, I found out she had been

seeing another man. I was furious. She blamed it on me. She said I wasn't making enough time for her, which I suppose was true enough. What with my duties in the hospital, the patients and spending time with my family also. It was challenging, but I'd attempted as best I could to make as much time with her as possible. I'd wanted as much time with her as possible. She began to make excuses not to see me. I grew suspicious. I followed her one night and found her with some pretty-boy Hollywood actor on the beach. I was shocked and crestfallen. I'd challenged them and *she* was furious. She said she never wanted to see me again. I tried to win her back, but to no avail. I was heartbroken, if I'm honest about it. Heartbroken like some childish high school student. I'd not seen her since, she ignored all my correspondence. Then eight days ago, she let herself into my office by my private door, while I was working late. She demanded I give her an abortion. I refused of course, I didn't do those types of things anymore, I protested. I hadn't done those things for a long time. I'd stopped. However, she threatened me, she said she'd tell my wife and children. I didn't know what to do. She was hysterical. I told her that she could keep the baby, that I'd support her. I'd find a way to make it work. She said it would ruin her life. She was most adamant she didn't want another child."

"Whose baby was it?" I asked. My voice unstable.

"She didn't know. Mine. Yours. The Hollywood actor's. A friend's. She just didn't know."

"How far along was she?"

"I don't know. I'm no Obstetrician, nor a Gynecologist. However, I'd surmise that Jean was perhaps a lot more than a few weeks into the first trimester, towards the end of it even, which I'd calculated possibly eliminated me as a potential father to the child."

I sank back into the seat. Punch drunk. I sobbed, my fist in my mouth, my teeth cutting into my skin. The Doc stopped talking for a moment. After a little while he continued.

"She wanted the procedure done that very night. In my office of all places. I refused still, but she again threatened to tell my wife and children, unless I did what she wanted that night. She said she'd just been offered a leading role in a film and needed the procedure done right away. You both had a lot in common, Kelly. You both were exceedingly good at extorting what you needed from others by using their weaknesses against them. Jean didn't need to extort me, because I loved her. I would have done anything for her. But she extorted me anyway. Strong armed me, therefor, unwillingly, I acquiesced. I attempted to prepare as best I could, sedated her heavily with chloroform and then started to perform the procedure. My hands were trembling I was under so much pressure. She had undergone sedation relatively well. But then, she, she began to hemorrhage badly, very badly, I'd done something wrong. Something had gone so very wrong. She… She lost so much blood. Too much. I didn't know what to do. She died there in my office like that. In my office on my consulting table, she just bled out while sedated. She never knew what happened. It was an accident, but I killed my love. I killed my love," he started weeping hard into his hands. Tremors ripped through his body as he continued his confession.

"I wrapped her up in sheets and waited until the early hours of the morning. Put her here in this very automobile, in the trunk, of all places. I drove to the harbor; took her body out to sea using my yacht and I… God forgive me… I put her in the water. Let her go into the waves. Watched her sink. Wrapped in sheets. I watched her sink. Watched her disappear… God forgive me. I killed my beloved. I killed her."

I wept brutally and silent, biting into my fist again and again, swallowing blood. Tremors ripped through my body as they had The Doc's.

"You're going to kill me now. I've known it all along. Please, just do it quickly. Please, just leave my body where it can be found. I don't want my children to think I deserted them. I want them to know I didn't leave them and their mother. I don't want them to question. Please. That's all I ask. Please."

"You mean, like you did to Jean? Her daughter will always

have questions. Jean's daughter will always wonder if her mother deserted her. What about her? And what about Jean's family? You selfish kraut fuck."

"I know. I know. I didn't know what else to do. I panicked. God forgive me, I panicked."

"That's not good enough, Doc," I picked up the pistol again and placed it against the side of his head. The pistol shaking and shuddering in my fist. Squeezing down on the trigger.

"Every time I close my eyes, I see her face. She's in my dreams. My nightmares. My wife awakes me in the night, saying I'm screaming and scaring the children. Hallucinations. The most vivid memories. In my office. This automobile. There are triggers everywhere. It's absolute misery. I can't live a normal life now, not knowing what I've done. If you're going to kill me, Kelly, just get it over with because I'm tired. So very, very tired," he removed his spectacles and rubbed at his eyes like a man who hadn't slept in days. Maybe he was telling the truth and he hadn't.

"Get out of the Cadillac, Doc."

He began to sob again. But not the begging kind of sobbing, or the pitiful kind of sobbing. I'd seen that kind of sobbing before in the war with some Jap prisoners, when we would line them up over large pits. It was the kind of sobbing someone did because they knew it was their time to die and there was no way out of it. 'Acceptance crying', we'd called it in Okinawa. They were crying for all the things they would never see and never do. The sobbing of someone who has finally realized they would never see their children grow into adults or their wives grow old. The sobbing of someone with so much more left to do. The Doc got out of the Cadillac, stumbled to his knees, stood up and gazed at the black Pacific Ocean weeping still and I got out and looked too. The smell and sound of it everywhere. I could focus on the ocean properly for the first time in years. I wondered how such a beautiful ocean had given me so many fears and so much anguish? Now Jean was somewhere out there in that same dark ocean, asleep and carried by the cold currents. I waved the pistol at The Doc grasping the rag to my face out of habit more than anything else.

"Turn around. Start walking, Doc."

"Where?"

"Just start walking down the road."

"Please, just make it quick."

"Shut the fuck up and walk."

He had his hands in the air like he was surrendering. I didn't know why.

I breathed in the ocean air and prepared myself for the hacking and the coughs, but none came. Maybe my lungs were finally empty of blood and mucus. I let him walk a few paces down the dirt track alongside the road and then I hobbled to the edge of the picnic area and stared down again at the jagged ocean below, I glanced down at the silhouette of the 1911 Colt pistol in my palsied hand and then lobbed it into the water. The splash a dull thudding sound. Then, I got back into the Cadillac, started the engine, and drove off leaving The Doc walking with his hands up in surrender in the darkness, surrounded by the sounds and smells of the Pacific Ocean and Jean's final resting place.

CHAPTER 12

THE BAR WAS dark like the ocean had been when I pulled the Cadillac up to the curb outside. I wiped at my wet stinging eyes with the crusty rag, turned the ignition off and slowly got out of the automobile. The avenue was still, the bar seemed dead to the world. An empty shell. Didn't seem so long ago I'd strolled down this avenue with Jean. Her high heels making song as she walked with her arm wrapped in mine, the smell of her perfume trailing behind us. Now the avenue was quiet, and Jean was dead. She was dead, although she wasn't gone. She would never really be gone. A woman like her could never really die. She'd merged now and become one with the L.A. avenues and streets. An immortal part of California for always. The newly refurbished Hollywood sign up on the hills a grave marker. The whole city had become a shrine to her. I couldn't stay here anymore. Every day would ache too much. I needed to leave this place.

I pushed at the bar door and it gave way, creaking open slightly. Charlie had forgotten to lock up. I'd have to warn the kid about that. It was an invitation for a robbery. I felt lightheaded and faint as I stepped into the gloomy dimness of the bar. Charlie wasn't there. Even in the darkness I could see that the place was even more of a mess than it had been the day before. I dragged myself over to the bar, went behind it and knocked on the back-room door. No answer and no sound of movement when I put my ear to the cool smoothness of it. Too weak, too exhausted to shout. I'd come back to the bar to tell Charlie he could have the deed to the place, it was his. I didn't care what he did with it. A gift from me to him. I wanted to pack some things and get the last of my cash from the safe. I'd decided on the drive back to the bar, I was going to New

York City. If I could make it, I'd check myself into a hospital up there and when I was better, I'd get a place nearby to my daughter, see her on the weekends, hopefully. Watch her grow up. Be a part of her life. I'd made a mistake letting her go, but it wasn't too late to fix it. I didn't want it to be too late to fix things. It wasn't too late for me, if I could just make it to New York. I realized that now. Hell, maybe I'd even try writing again.

The mantel clock on the shelf behind the bar chimed twelves times. It had become Sunday. Billie Holiday's voice floated into my mind. Gloomy Sunday. I returned to the bar and poured myself a shot of whisky. Switched on the bar lights. The bulbs illuminated slowly, flickered, casting a sickly yellow light over the shadows and that was when I saw Charlie. Sickly, yellow Charlie. Sat at the table by the window. Just sat there, eyes narrowed into slits, mouth screwed up into an ugly sneer. He had a look on him I'd seen before. I remembered then. When he was shooting dice. I'd seen it in Okinawa at the end of the war. A twisted, spiteful face that made me feel disgust and hate at the same time.

IT WAS AFTER the island of Okinawa had been completely taken by the American Forces. After our war was meant to have been won. The remaining Japanese had surrendered or committed seppuku, ritual suicide. The atmosphere had changed almost overnight and there was an overwhelming feeling of relief. A somber kind of elation among the platoon. Holed up in a destroyed village in the South of the island, waiting to be relieved, so we could march back to the coast, catch a boat ride towards home and loved ones. The only enemies we had left to face down were boredom and the sobering, painful realization of the things we had done to other human beings. Things we'd done to survive. Things we'd done out of hate, fear and spite.

There was a sugarcane field growing next to the village's remains. Long sheafs of the deepest green growing up to my shoulders. The small field was left completely unspoiled by the war somehow. So much of the village was heavily damaged, broken down into nothing recognizable, but that green field had remained virgin. Before I finally left the island, I would walk through that field at night, under the moonlight, my Thompson slung over my back, defunct, and I would run my hands over the tops of all that luscious green, surrounded by the sweetest scent. It was the closest I'd been to at peace in a long, long time.

One afternoon before we were shipped out, the children of the village were running though the long leaves of the sugar, playing a game of hide and seek. Playing and giggling like children anywhere in the world. In all that green they could lose themselves in nature and for a little while forget all the things they'd witnessed and endured. All the blood and all the pain. After all the hurt, killing and misery, these children could still laugh and play. They amazed me with their little, white smiles. I sat watching them for a little over an hour, smoking in the shade of a broken wall. They'd run up to me, panting, out of breath, smiling and I would offer them chewing gum, they'd take some and then run off, disappearing again into the long storks of the emerald field. I'd unslung my Thompson, leant it against the rubble I'd been perched on and went into the lush greenery to play with them. To try and forget too for a little while. I acted the fool, pretending to be a monster. Chasing them, tickling them softly and they ran screaming from me, the happy kind of children's screaming that I hadn't heard one time throughout the whole bullshit war. It made me feel happy, content and the more they laughed and the more they screamed with joy the more I clowned around and the happier I felt too. The more I could lose myself there. The children had found a small fragment of heaven on that island and they let me into it. An island of heaven in an ocean of hell.

I'd wanted to get a few of the other Marines from my platoon to come over and play with the kids too, so I jogged back through the crumbling village to get a small group together. There were a few guys here and there sat around smoking, dozing, or drinking and I let them know. Pointed the way, wanting to share the special place the children and I'd found, but they just shrugged their shoulders and carried on smoking, dozing, or drinking. I went deeper into the ruined streets until I found a gang of Marines standing around in a close circle, they were whooping and hollering. Shooting dice. I'd always enjoyed shooting dice and it was always a good way to pass the time then. I strolled over and pushed my way through the group. The crowd went quiet. The hollering faded and Marines quickly began to disperse and scatter. Then I saw Charlie on the ground. I thought he was doing push-ups. His pants were down showing his bare, pale, spotty ass. What the fuck is this idiot doing now? I'd thought. Then I'd glimpsed the small thin legs pushed out and pressed down by Charlie's hips and weight. He was ripping, tearing into the thing again and again. I acted intuitively, kicking him as hard as I could with the toe of my boot to the ribs. He hollered, rolled off, pulling up his pants and then I saw the tiny little Japanese girl, not yet old enough to have even started puberty. In the dry dirt and dust just staring at nothing, like she was dead. I only realized she was still alive when she started whimpering in my arms as I carried her away, back to the villagers. Disgusted and revolted, I'd looked back at Charlie, squinted into the sun seeing his sneering face contorted into a mess of meanness, sickness, and hate.

THE SAME FACE he glared at me with now. Charlie, he'd come back from Okinawa so infected with memories, he was even more tormented than I was. I'd shit all over my life, but I'd known love at least. Jean had loved me. I'd felt it. I'd known it. I had a daughter that would remember me holding her in my arms one day, remember that I did love her too. Charlie had nothing. Nothing but awful memories and a cot in the back of this piss stinking bar. I should have tried to help him more, the poor sick bastard.

He stood there trembling, breathing heavily, panting like a

sick dog across the bar from me. He reminded me of a pet mongrel we'd had when I was eleven years old. It had gone missing one day and we'd found it out by the railway tracks, its guts spread out by its flayed, torn open stomach. Still alive somehow and its eyes rolling around in its head. Growling, frothing thickly at the mouth and when I'd knelt down to comfort it, as it lay dying, it had snapped its jaws down onto my hand, drawing blood.

"Charlie..." I said.

His fist exploded in a blinding flash of light. I was knocked back against the front of the bar hard. Fell to the floor. My stomach like shards of ice. All the air ripped from my lungs. I looked up at the cruel face. Charlie was gone. I didn't know the person he was. I'd never known.

"Have I got the fuckin' gumption now, Lieutenant Scott?!" he screamed triumphantly.

"Who is the sissy now, Lieutenant Scott?! Who's the fuckin' sissy now!?" he whooped.

I didn't understand. Couldn't breathe. Smelt iron and shit. Sucked in dusty, smoky air. Coughed. Hacked. Wheezed.

"Why, Charlie?"

"Why?! Why?! You made me bury those Nips! Those fuckin' Nips, I couldn't kill. You made me bury em'. You humiliated me. You fuckin' humiliated me in front of the whole fuckin' platoon! They called me a queer behind my back! I know it! You made me a fuckin' laughingstock, Lieutenant Scott. That's why! That's why! And now the bar's mine. They said I could have it and now it's mine."

"Who, Charlie?"

Then the scent of blood and shit faded, and I could smell a sweet aroma all around me. Thought I heard a voice somewhere in the room. Calling to me. The sound was muffled, faint, but I thought I heard it coming from somewhere not too far off. I opened my palms by my sides and imagined I could feel the soft brush of the tips of sugar cane.

Charlie stumbled towards me. I saw the muzzle pointed towards my right eye. My right eye ached.

"You were right, Lieutenant Scott. You don't call them. They call you..."

And then his fist burst so bright, it looked like a star going supernova...

EPILOGUE

Los Angeles October 1953

HE STILL WALKED with a limp. His knee had a throbbing dull ache in its core since the long maddening boat ride back to Los Angeles had reached its midway point. His knee always felt this way just before it rained. He looked up, but it was still a clear afternoon. Not a cloud in the blue sky. Must have been the ocean air. He thought he should have listened to his wife, Maggie, and brought his cane with him, but it hindered him nowadays. Made him feel like an old cripple.

He'd always disliked walking with the cane and he'd always disliked this fucking town. Los Angeles. It had always seemed fake to him. Everything appeared as though it was made of papier-mâché and pine frames. One big Hollywood film set full of actors, actresses and extras in a movie with a bad script and no understandable plot. It'd been exactly four years since he'd left this city and it hadn't changed all that much. He'd changed a lot. For the worse. He was still alive and breathing, but too much had been taken from him. Too much pain. Too much sorrow. They had come for him first in New York City. They had tried to kill him in Boston, but he had adapted quickly. A lot of men had died. He was still alive; he'd changed and now he was back, and he'd seen L.A hadn't changed all that much. It wasn't much of a reunion. He'd planned to come back earlier to see Mickey Cohen, but the government had saved the piece of shit's life and got him on tax evasion. Tony was in Vegas and unreachable. No, it wasn't much of a reunion at all.

He had spent the morning walking around the old town, remembering things he thought he'd forgotten. Eaten half an ice cream cone on a bench by the Santa Monica Pier and sent a couple of postcards to his wife and kids back in Hawaii. Now as he walked down the avenue, a brown paper bag gently swinging in one hand, he ran the fingers of the other hand through his grey streaked, red, wavy hair. Thinking about what souvenirs would make his children happiest. So far, he'd just seen the usual, run of the mill, tacky souvenirs and he wanted to get them something special each. They had all been through so much shit the last couple of years. Endured too much. Endured more than any children should. Too much. Maggie, too. She'd aged so quickly since New York. She smiled rarely nowadays, but when she did it always illuminated his world. Maybe, the snow globes with the Hollywood sign inside. No, not good enough. He didn't know. He was always bad at picking out presents, he normally left that up to Maggie, she was always great at that kind of thing.

At the end of the avenue, he came up on the bar at last. The sign above the door was broken and missing half of its gold letters, so it just read 'K•L••'S BA•'. The front windows were boarded up with plywood. A cardboard sign taped to the entrance door had the word 'CLOSED' scrawled on it in childish writing. He pushed on the door and it creaked open slightly, releasing an unpleasant, filthy odor much worse than the usual bar smells. He could see a dim light through the opened slit, so he pushed the door open wider and stepped into the damp shadows. The smell of filth was stronger inside and he could see why; empty bottles in disarray along the mahogany bar and piles of wadded toilet paper, empty tomato cans, newspapers and Chinese takeaway boxes piled knee high on the tiled flooring here and there. The bar had probably been very beautiful at one time, he could tell by the ornate carpentry of the bar and furniture and the colorful stained glass inlaid into the dark, rich wood. Someone had put a lot of time and effort into creating a touch of the Emerald Isle in this place, but now it was just a stinking dump, in disrepair and decay. What a fucking waste, he thought sadly. He squinted his eyes at the bar and thought he saw a rat scamper across it by the man who was reading a comic or something by the one bulb of light that still appeared to work in the place.

"Hey, Mister, you open?" he called out softly.

The man at the bar, a greasy and jaundice faced figure wearing a dirty vest, with large scabs on his head, probably from shaving his scalp, startled and almost fell off his chair.

"Shit! What do you want? We're closed. Closed. Didn't you read the sign on the door?"

"I'm sorry, Mister. I've been travelin' a long time and I'm just thirsty, I guess."

The mangy figure stood up straight and slapped his comic book down on the bar top making a dismal, unthreatening thump.

"I said, we are closed. You deaf as well as stupid?"

"Could I just have a shot of gin, seein' as I'm here now, you're here now and I've got the dough, if you've got the liquor?" the man took a silver money clip out of the breast pocket of his gaudy Hawaiian shirt and flashed it in the air.

"Well, seeings as you got the cash, one drink shouldn't hurt none," said the barkeep. He rooted around underneath the bar and brought out an almost empty bottle of gin, then found an empty shot glass on the shelf behind him and poured the drink on the cluttered bar top. The man in the Hawaiian shirt sat down at a stool in front of the mahogany bar, flicking a dead cockroach off of the cushioned seat as he did and placed the paper bag he'd been carrying on the stool beside him. He passed the skinny, jaundiced barkeep a five spot, which disappeared into a grubby pair of slacks without any offer of change.

"My name's Rudy," the man in the Hawaiian shirt said, sticking out his palm and the other man took it, shook it limply with a damp, clammy hand.

"I'm Lieutenant Charlie."

"Lieutenant, huh? You were in the war?"

"Yes, Sir, I was. The Marines. Killed about a hundred of them dirty Nips in Okinawa during the war, I did."

"Really?"

"Yep, that's a fact. I got the Purple Heart and everything."

"Is that a fact?"

"Yeah. It's a fact. Why? You don't believe me? You think I

look like the kind of person to make things up?"

"No, I'm just makin' conversation is all. Nice, cozy little bar, you got here. It's yours, is it?"

"Yeah, it's mine. Why you ask?" Charlie said.

"I just wondered."

"You just wondered, huh? What are you some kind of detective? Why you in town, anyway? Business trip or some such bullshit, I'll bet my bottom dollar."

"I'm back in town to do a favor for an old friend. He died a few years back," Rudy said lifting the glass to his mouth and finishing it with a flick of the wrist.

"Is that so? Well, you've finished your drink, so you should beat it now, before I get all agitated and you wouldn't like that, trust me. Killed about a hundred Nips I have. You wouldn't like it if I got agitated with you, no sir. You can bet your bottom dollar on that."

Rudy slid off the barstool slowly and stood up straight, looking at the mongrel like figure behind the bar.

"Ah, that reminds me. I've got something for you, Lieutenant Charlie," Rudy said, placing the paper bag on the bar and motioning for Charlie to look inside. Charlie reached in the bag and brought out a carton of milk, placed it sullenly on the bar.

"Milk? Why the heck would I want a carton of milk?" Charlie said scratching his shaved head and staring down at the carton.

"It's a private joke from a story the old friend told me about," Rudy said as he placed the revolver against Charlie's forehead and fired. The flash illuminated the place. A flash of lightning. Charlie flew against the back of the bar shaking it violently and knocking some pint glasses down smashing to the floor. Rudy casually walked behind the bar and fired three more rounds into Charlie, returned the revolver back to the pocket of his slacks and walked out of Kelly's into the bright sunlight of a Los Angeles afternoon, still wondering what souvenirs he should buy for his family. Maybe, the snow globes would be okay after all.

Acknowledgments & Thanks

First and foremost, I would like to say thank you to a few people who championed and aided my work from the very beginning. Moy McCrory, my university professor who told me to keep writing. Brian 'Zygote in My Coffee' Fuggett for being the first editor that I submitted my poetry to. Laura Hird for being there from day one. Rob 'Blackstoke' Parker for always being there to help a struggling author out. Sean Coleman who took a chance on a stray that occasionally pisses on the rug. Martine, Barbara, Scott, James, Nate, Kirstyn, Max, Travis, Gabriel, John BN, Alec PM and Kev for your efforts, support and aid in proofreading and editing.

I would like to say an incredibly special thank you to those whose constant love, support and help were indispensable to me throughout my writing.

My daughters M and N for letting papa write when you wanted to play.

M for being M. Just keep watching!

Mother and Father, Family.

Friends.

Okinawa! I love you!

R.I.P Jean Spangler

The authors, editors, reviewers, bloggers, and beta readers who have helped me throughout. You know who you are. Much love. Thank you.

And **thanks to YOU** the reader!

Stephen J. Golds
July 2021

About the Author

Stephen J. Golds was born in London, U.K, but has lived in Japan for most of his adult life. He enjoys spending time with his daughters, reading books, traveling, boxing, and listening to old Soul LPs. His novels are Say Goodbye When I'm Gone, Always the Dead, I'll Pray When I'm Dying, Poems for Ghosts in Empty Tenement Windows, Cut-throat & Tongue-tied Bullet Riddled & Gun Shy and the story and poetry collection Love Like Bleeding Out with an Empty Gun in Your Hand. He is co-Editor of Punk Noir Magazine.

CPSIA information can be obtained
at www.ICGtesting.com
Printed in the USA
LVHW090312290921
698984LV00003B/178